Lost at the End of the World

Lost at the End of the World

Rupert Attlee

Hindon Publishing

First published in Great Britain by Hindon Publishing 2021

Illustrations drawn by the pupils of Sandroyd School

A CIP catalogue record of this book is available from the British Library.

ISBN 978-7399285-0-6

Design & Typesetting by Geoff Fisher
geoff.fisher@yahoo.co.uk

Printed in Bound in Great Britain by
CPI Group (UK) Ltd, Croydon CR0 4YY

HINDON PUBLISHING
Willowbrook
Watery Lane
Donhead St Mary
Shaftesbury
SP7 9DP

To all pupils I have ever taught for your
constant inspiration
To fellow adventurers, Michael & David
Above all, to my daughters, Indie & Flo

*'The more you knew of South America, the more you would
understand that anything was possible – anything.'*
SIR ARTHUR CONAN DOYLE 'The Lost World'

CONTENTS

Foreword

The End of the World is a place that dreams are made of...

Mysterious. Mystical. And, at times, just plain Weird. Unlike 'Narnia' and 'Middle Earth', it is a real place, sitting at the southernmost tip of South America. This region is often referred to as Patagonia – the Land of Giants.

It is not a place you would choose to be lost in, even in your wildest dreams. Towering mountains, thundering glaciers and erupting volcanoes block your path, and if these obstacles are not enough, the weather is extreme – ferocious seas, bone-chilling cold and howling gales.

You will not be surprised to know that very few people live in this untamed wilderness. But you will find you are not alone... As you seek your way out, you will sense you are being watched. A flicker of movement out of the corner of your eye, an uprush of air above your head. The End of the World is home to some of the strangest and toughest animals and birds on the planet. They know how to survive and you need to trust them if you are going to make it out alive...

I am writing this story having once been Lost at the End of the World.

Chapter 1 – Rounding the Horn

The sea was the colour of milk. Waves, whipped by the howling wind, bulged and surged. Without mercy, time and time again they pounded the sides of the ship, causing her to lurch dangerously from side to side. The sky above was bruised and low and heavy with foreboding.

On the deck, at the very nose of the ship, stood a boy. He clung to the cold metal railings, knuckles white, knees alternatively flexing and bracing as he rode the heaving deck. The salty spray stung his blue eyes and whipped his blond hair into a tangled mess. As he squinted into the gathering darkness, he could just make out the shadowy, looming form of Cape Horn. At its heart, he spied a flickering, white light. Then a giant wave reared up before him, breaking across the tilting deck, and suddenly the light he had seen vanished, together with the grey, ominous form of the Horn.

Jack shivered with fear and exhilaration. He had never been more scared in his life, but at the same time, he had never felt so free – no one to tell him what to do, how to behave and pour cold water on his adventurous spirit. For the time being at least, there was no more, *'Jack, you can't do that!'* Or *'Jack, don't even think about it.'* Nagging, disparaging remarks that had plagued him all his life. But now there was no one around to

scream, *"Jack, come below deck now. It's a raging storm out there."*

Jack seemed immune to the numbing cold. For years he had dreamt of rounding the Horn – the Everest of the sailing world, the ultimate challenge and, at the same time, a ships' graveyard. The Horn was in an angrier mood than Jack had ever dreamt or ever could have imagined. The books he had read had failed to conjure up this assault on the senses – the howling wind, the biting spray, the seething cauldron of boiling water, the smell and taste of fear and excitement.

Below deck, in a small passenger cabin away from the shrieking wind, a young boy ran excitedly up and down the heaving aisle, occasionally swinging between the seats. Seemingly oblivious to the storm outside, he was singing at the top of his voice:

"Row, Row, Row your boat
Gently down the stream.

Merrily, Merrily, Merrily, Merrily
Life is but a dream."

He was soon adding an array of animal noises to accompany the song's unfolding drama: first a squeak at the mention of a mouse, then a scream as he mimicked the jaws of a crocodile, before rounding off the performance with a great roar of a lion.

It wasn't long before his singing was getting on the nerves of the other passengers. A pale-faced girl staring out the window seemed to be the closest at reaching the end of her tether.

"Can't you like tell him to shut up?" she snapped, her face pinched in irritation.

Another girl of a similar age, sitting across the aisle, looked up dreamily. She had the same high cheekbones and slanting eyebrows as the young boy.

"Yes, no, there's nothing wrong with singing," she said in a matter-of-fact voice.

"You call that singing? Singing...it's more like demented shrieking!" Her pale face was turning red in frustration and anger.

Flo did not rise to the bait. "What would you prefer, singing or crying? Ben's only eight and he could well be blubbering in my arms. Please let him be."

"Anything would be better than that like squeaking, screaming and roaring. Can't he play quietly?" huffed Bella. She crossed her arms and her mouth twisted like she had just eaten a lemon. Her shoulders rose and her neck drooped in a dramatic sulk. A minute later, she sighed and reached for her red, patent leather handbag. Out came a nail file, and she started to file her nails. Despite having to look down, her nose seemed to be still poking up into the air.

Amidst the mayhem, Flo was turning greener and greener. Her face was starting to match the colour of her green eyes. For her brother Ben's sake, she was trying to look her usual cool and relaxed self. Inside, however, her heart was beating like an orchestra of drums and her stomach was turning somersaults. She shivered as she looked out through the circular port-hole. Spray whipped the glass and the sea was a cauldron of white.

Outside, Jack had not moved from the bow. Legs astride, he stood staring across the menacing sea. It was dark now and he could just make out the flashing, blurred light of Cape Horn. '*We must be west of the Horn by now,* he thought, *surely soon we will be turning north up the coast of Chile into calmer waters.*' He looked up at the sky and, at that very moment, the clouds parted to reveal a crescent moon. This had to be a good sign. He prayed silently for the storm to finally relent.

Down below, Ben stopped singing and started to chase a plastic water bottle up and down the aisle. He had a mischievous grin, and it was clear that he knew what buttons to press to annoy people. This grin was combined with a quizzical look, which gave him an air of innocence – a permanent "What me?" question appeared pasted on his lips. He resembled the Artful

Dodger, without the jaunty top hat and tails, but with all the swagger and self-confidence. From top to toe, Ben was unkempt – his brown hair was a tangled mess, his shirt hung loosely out of his trousers, his shoes were scuffed and his laces undone. He had a high-pitched, squeaky voice, which could test the patience and nerves of even the most relaxed person. If Ben was a dog, he would be a Jack Russell.

By contrast, his elder sister, Flo, just turned 13, was a dreamer. If she were a sweet, she would be a curly wurly. Staring with green distant eyes, she seemed to drift in and out consciousness. She had the air of an artist with tousled blonde hair, a colourful floral shirt and extravagantly flared striped trousers. She did nothing quickly and her movements were slow and measured. Her voice mirrored her movements – quiet, lilting and barely more than a whisper. There was a calmness about her, which helped when dealing with her younger brother. She tried to take her mind off her churning stomach by trying to remember the words of the poem, 'Daffodils' by William Wordsworth. She had won the school poetry recital competition with this poem.

"I wandered lonely as a cloud
That floats on high o'er vales and hills...
The waves beside them danced, but they
Out-did the sparkling waves in glee."

Flo paused. She looked out through the porthole.

Those were not dancing, sparkling waves, they were menacing and angry.

Across the aisle, Bella, her face pinched with concentration and determination, was now attempting to paint her nails. Unsurprisingly, she was not happy with the results. Blotchy colours and tattered wobbly lines. But she had succeeded in taking her mind off the mayhem outside. The lights flickered, the floor shook, the tables trembled, a door banged and they were plunged into darkness. With a disgruntled sigh, she dropped the nail varnish into her bag.

Bella was irritated. Ben and the storm were only partially to blame – she possessed a permanent state of disapproval, unhappiness and irritation. Laughter did not come naturally to her and she only tended to smile at someone's misfortune. Private school education and stern, hug-adverse parents made Bella believe that showing emotion, being spontaneous and taking risks were weaknesses. This left her aloof and angry, and was reflected by her choice of clothes – a scarlet shirt with a sharp raised collar. Her jet-black hair was swept tightly back, and her eyes were small below her furrowed brow.

Up above, Jack thought how wrong he had been! Far from relenting, the storm had now reached fever pitch. The wind screamed like a banshee, and clouds scudded at a frightening pace across the fragile moon. The waves tossed the stricken ship from side to side. She groaned, creaked and whimpered.

High on the bridge, Captain Hawkins looked down

on the lonely figure riding the waves at the bow. He could see himself in that lone boy. At his age, he had done the same. From that very place, he had experienced the freedom and exhilaration of the sea, waves and wind and marvelled at the sheer power of nature. This was when his love affair with the ocean had started, and now a veteran of five Horns and thousands of nautical miles, he had made a career from the sea. Fleetingly, he envied the boy, unburdened as he was with responsibility. As Captain, he now had decisions to make. In all his time at sea, he had never seen conditions like this before.

His ship, his old girl, was struggling to stay alive in the face of this onslaught. The tremors and shudders below his feet were like nails being driven through his heart. He could feel her suffering as she bravely fought to stay afloat. *'Come on old girl, tough it out'* he pleaded under his breath. He sensed a looming shadow behind. Slowly, he turned to see an immense wave. A black, roaring wall of water topped with white surf bearing down on the stricken ship. *'She is going to be swallowed up...'* A sea of water crashed against the windows of the bridge.

The ship was knocked sideways. Floored, she seemed down and out, and then miraculously she rose to her feet again. Water cascaded off her decks and Captain Hawkins could just make out the boy scrambling across the deck and clinging frantically to the iron railings. Another wave crashed against her, sending her reeling back towards the hungry sea. She let out a wounded, agonising groan and almost immediately the hum of the engines died. Her heart had stopped.

"MAYDAY, MAYDAY, MAYDAY. The Maria Louise sinking. The Maria Louise sinking. Latitude -55 58'28.19 S Longitude -67 16' 10.80 W. 18 people aboard, 14 crew and 4 passengers. OVER." The Captain spoke rapidly into the VHS radio. Captain Hawkins then gave the order to abandon ship.

The children could not fail to notice that the engines had stopped. The metal door clanged open. Clad in bright yellow oil skins, a sailor stood silhouetted in the doorway. Ben stopped his singing and playing.

"You must go up to the top deck now!" ordered the sailor, struggling to hold his balance.

Sensing the urgency in the sailor's voice, Flo rose to her feet, and Ben ran to embrace her like a limpet. Bella did not move but nonchalantly continued to inspect her nails.

"I'm not going. It's all like windy and wet up there," Bella said petulantly.

"Captain's orders," the sailor replied dismissively.

Bella slowly packed away her nail file in her red, patent leather handbag and rose up slowly. Once standing, she tilted her head up to stick her nose in the air.

"Quick! hurry up! I haven't the time to faff around. We must go now!" shouted the sailor in growing desperation and exasperation.

As if in answer, the floor trembled, rose, and tilted, forcing Flo to stumble and Ben to lose his grip around her neck. He screamed. Bella, nose still in the air and handbag in hand, was sent sprawling down the aisle between the green, plastic seats. Flo could not resist a wry smile. The ship let out a long, agonising groan.

The sailor led them slowly up the iron stairs. While Flo and Ben clung frantically to the handrail to keep their balance, Bella attempted to ascend elegantly like a model on a catwalk. Who was she trying to impress? Each step of the iron stairs was alive, pitching up and down, to the right and left. After the fourth step, Bella was also clinging to the handrail but still clutching her handbag.

The sailor forced open the heavy steel door. A blast of freezing, biting air hit him, sending him stumbling backwards. Flo, Ben and Bella heard the roar of the wind a split second before it punched them in the face. They struggled out onto the heaving deck. The sea was in chaos. Milky white in the pale moonlight, hissing and spitting, striking against the side of the struggling ship. A blurred shadow close to the iron railing turned to face them. Jack's eyes were wide with excitement and fear.

They had met for the first time in Buenos Aires just 10 days before. Fate had forced them together, to share the voyage from Argentina to the Chilean city of Punta Arenas. They were the children of British diplomats. With growing hostilities between Britain and Argentina, adult '*wisdom*' had considered it '*safer*' to send them around the Horn to Chile to attend the British school in Punta Arenas. So, while the adults toughed it out in the Argentine capital, the children were left to weather this storm.

It is fair to say that they were still strangers and far from becoming friends. Ben was just eight years old and, like most boys his age, he was curious, loud, had questionable hygiene and had yet to learn how to blow his nose. His sister, Flo, appeared dreamy and poetic, but inside she possessed a steely determination. Above all, she was kind and caring. Jack was the eldest at 15. At school he conformed, and his teachers would refer to him as a model pupil. He liked to see himself differently - as fiercely independent, brave and an adventurer. Bella was just a year younger than Jack, and she was obsessed with just one person – herself. She spent the majority of her time looking in the mirror, applying make-up and whinging. Whinging about the food, the hardness of the beds, the constant smell of diesel and the angry state of the sea. It was not hard to see why the children (and they were the only children on the ship) had not become the best of friends and chosen instead largely to ignore each other.

Their differences and dislike were certainly on their minds as the sailor led them towards one of the life rafts. The ship was claustrophobic enough with little space to avoid each other, but the life raft!

The sea was plunging and lunging, writhing and seething, rising and falling. The rain was lashing down from the bruised and leaden sky. It felt like the roof of the world was collapsing above their heads as the lightning jabbed and stabbed at the restless sea. Waves smashed against the sides of the ship sending up plumes of spray. Thunder-like cannon fire boomed above the incessant roar of the waves. Thunder and lightning merged as one.

"To the life raft!" screamed the sailor. The children teetered across the foaming, heaving deck. They struggled to keep their balance as the ship seemed intent on throwing them off, like a wild horse experiencing a saddle and rider for the first time. The ship bucked violently. They clung to rails and groped for ropes as they crawled and danced their way towards the swinging life raft.

Bella was taking longer than the others. She only had one hand free, in the other she still clutched her red handbag as if her life depended on it.

"For pity's sake, get rid of that bag!" commanded the sailor, struggling to be heard above the roar of the ocean. Bella looked startled. The thought of losing her bag was more frightening than the storm raging around them. When she finally made it to the life raft, the exasperated sailor grabbed the bag and threw it over the side. At first, the bag popped up and woobled like a weeble. Another wave broke and swallowed the bag up. A piercing scream rose above the roaring waves and thunder. Lightning ripped through the sky and Jack could just make out the horror on Bella's mascara-streaked face.

There were two sailors now on the heaving deck. One on each rope, they steadily lowered the boat into the menacing sea.

"Jump in. Now!" ordered the sailor on the bow rope. Jack jumped gingerly down. He looked up and reached up to help Flo, twinned with Ben clutching frantically around her neck. Bella, ever the Princess, refused any help and attempted to step elegantly aboard. Just as she jumped, the boat twisted, sending her sprawling like a floundering mackerel. Seconds later, a huge wave smashed against the side of the ship and swallowed the life raft. The sailors lost control and the ropes whirled through the screaming iron pulleys.

Chapter 2 - Overboard

The life raft hit the sea. Water edged its way up the sides perilously close to the top. Just when all seemed lost, the raft steadied itself and bobbed up like a cork. Another wave hit them, sending them spiralling away from the looming shadow of the ship. The Maria Louise was listing at a precarious angle, and they watched in horror as the stern rose. The lights flickered defiantly, then vanished, plunging the ship into darkness. Soundlessly and steadily, the ship was swallowed and devoured by the hungry sea – taking 18 adult souls to a watery grave. They were now alone, heading off into the unknown.

The sea was a foaming cauldron. They were helpless as the life raft was tossed, turned and twisted. Time and time again, the life raft rose to the crest of a wave only to be sent plunging back down again. It was a roller coaster to beat all roller coasters, only there was no end in sight.

"I feel like dizzy!" screamed Bella.

"I am cold," shivered Flo through chattering teeth.

Ben was jabbering into Flo's shoulder, inaudible above the roar of the waves.

Amid the chaos, Jack liked the fact he was the eldest. All his life he had obeyed and listened to others, now was his chance to take responsibility and be listened to.

He attempted to reassure the others. "I have just seen the Horn -it's was not far away. What's more this storm cannot last forever."

As if in answer, a huge wave sent the life raft spiralling into the air. This was no time for talking. The silence was deafening as the children clung on for dear life, riding the waves as they were swept into gathering gloom.

After an hour that seemed like an eternity, the moon suddenly appeared, dropping low on the horizon, and on the other side of the world the morning sun rose and broke through the billowing clouds. The wind ceased its howling and started instead to whine. Waves now became less menacing and seemed to be guiding rather hurtling them towards the looming shadow of land. A strange glitter bubbled in the water around the sides of the life raft, and behind them these same sparkles of light fanned out like a peacock's tail. The children looked in amazement.

"Phosphorescence," said Jack. "I saw some once while on holiday in Cornwall. Nothing as amazing as this, though."

Hope filled the life raft and warmed their hearts. They watched a shadow glide across the luminous water. A lone albatross swooped down, white-tipped wings stretching three metres across, and fixed them with its beady eyes.

"What is that?" shouted Ben in a high-pitched voice, pointing at the sky. Instead of looking up at the sky, Bella stared at Ben in amazement. This was the first time that they had heard him speak rather than sing.

"That is one huge, strange-looking bird," said Flo.

"I think it's an albatross. It has to be a good sign," Jack whispered reassuringly. "Remember that poem 'The Rime of the Ancient Mariner'? They were doomed until the arrival of the albatross brought the sailors good luck. The winds suddenly started up from the south and they were able to sail away from the icebergs."

"Yes, I remember. I learnt part of the poem at school," said Flo dreamily.

> *"The ice was here, the ice was there,*
> *The ice was all around:*
> *It cracked and growled, and roared and howled,*
> *Like noises in a swound!"*

"Oh, do be quiet! Don't you like know anything?" said an exasperated Bella. "The albatross was a curse and the voyage ended in disaster with all the crew dying of some strange disease," she muttered. "What about the saying 'an albatross around your neck'?"

"Why would anyone hang that thing around their neck?" asked Ben incredulously.

"That is just like the point!" said Bella dismissively. "They don't."

"The bad luck came only after they shot the albatross," said Jack, bristling with irritation. "Served them right if you ask me. What sort of person would wish to kill such a majestic bird?"

As if in answer, the albatross swooped down and

landed on the bow of the life raft. It stretched its impressive wingspan, shaking the wetness out of each wing, before expertly folding them into its body. Up close, you could see the pinkish yellow of the hooked bill, the black, steely eyes and the mottled, grey-black plumage.

"Has it come to eat us?" stammered Ben.

"Don't be silly," whispered Flo. "It is just looking for some company. There can't be much of that at the End of the World."

It was then that it dawned upon them all that they really were at World's End. Cape Horn was the world's southernmost tip and Antarctica was less than 1,600 kilometres away. No wonder it was so freezing. The land that they could now faintly see through the mist was the island of Tierra del Fuego – the land of fire – sitting at the foot of Patagonia – a place named by Ferdinand Magellan after the big feet of its giant natives. A place of legend and mystery, peppered with dramatic landscapes, unforgiving weather and strange animals. Thoughts of this destination sent a collective shiver down their spines, apart from Ben, who sat in blissful ignorance having never heard of Tierra del Fuego or Patagonia. It was not so much the challenging nature of the place, it was the thought of having to survive together.

"He wants us to follow him!" exclaimed Jack excitedly. "He just flicked his head to one side."

"Are you out of your mind?" shrieked Bella.

"No. Trust me. Just look at those eyes."

Those eyes did look wise and reassuring.

"We have nothing to lose," said Flo supportively.

"I cannot believe I am hearing this. Following a bird, whatever next!" muttered Bella, full of contempt.

Bella's '*whatever next*' was drowned by the roar of breaking surf. Jagged rocks suddenly appeared to the right of them, to their left, ahead and behind them, just like the ice in 'The Rime of the Ancient Mariner'.

"Out with the paddles!" screamed Jack. At the same time, he reached down and attached the life raft's emergency pack to his arm with a Velcro strap.

None of them had ever been white water rafting before, but this was exactly how they imagined it to be. Surrounded by foaming, rushing water, sharp, piercing rocks, a cacophony of sound and plumes of spray stinging your eyes, while the raft swayed violently from side to side.

With one last knowing look, the albatross spread its wings and took off, rapidly beating its wings to gain height, before gliding and weaving its way through the maze of menacing rocks. The children paddled like crazy as they frantically tried to follow. Jack, with one eye on the albatross, shouted instructions, "To the right!" "Back paddle!" "All to the left!" Even Bella, forgetting the fragility of her nails, was getting stuck in as she sensed the urgency of the situation. Ben had detached himself from Flo and was stretching over the side to dip his paddle into the churning water. They slalomed their way through the jagged rocks that stood like gravestones in a cemetery. They followed in the ss, who kept looking back to check yond the rocks, they could just make ashing, thundering surf, and then a steep each.

We are close now," warned Jack. "Bring up the paddles and cling on!"

A wave swelled behind them, then suddenly rose like a cobra, hissing and foaming at the mouth. It hung above them for what seemed like an age, before striking them with a venomous spray. The life raft somersaulted, and they were thrown into the cold, angry sea. Jack felt like he was in a washing machine, turning time and time again head over heels. He was so dizzy he no longer knew which way was up or which way was down. With bursting lungs, he headed for the surface only to hit the pebbly bottom. He pushed upwards and broke through the surface, gasping for breath, only to be hit by another wave that sent him sprawling on to the shingle of the beach. The last thing he remembered was how freezing cold he was.

Chapter 3 – Elephant Beach

Jack awoke, feeling warm. The pebbles of the beach were digging into his back. With his eyes still closed and crusted with salt, he shifted to one side. He bumped into something soft and warm. He reached out one hand and felt a body of undulating gel. He could also feel warm breath caressing his face, and the air was full of tremulous snoring. Unnerved, he prised himself up on one elbow and in the gloomy dawn light he could make out a long, blubbery body with a mermaid tail at one end and a 40 cm snout at the other. He turned and there was another, just centimetres away. He sat up and as far as his eye could see was a snoring, sleeping colony of elephant seals.

Miraculously, the collective snoring of 50 elephant seals along with their body warmth had evaporated the freezing sea water from his clothes. He stood up and was relieved to find that the emergency kit had remained attached to his arm. Still disorientated by sleep, he imagined that the sixth seal to his right was talking. Not only that, it was speaking in English. How strange, surely they would speak Spanish or some Patagonian dialect. Or failing that Welsh but certainly not English.

"Help," groaned the seal. "Help."

The strained voice sounded familiar.

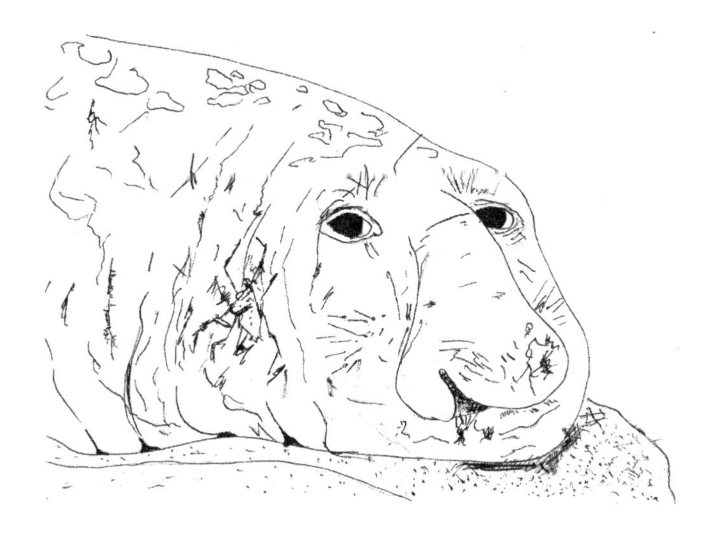

"Who's there," asked Jack tentatively.

"Like Bella, stupid. Who do you think?"

Jack did not have the courage to answer her question truthfully.

"My hands are stuck under this, like, stinking, snoring lump of blubber. For goodness' sake, get me out of here."

Fortunately for Jack, his laugh was drowned out by the snoring.

Jack stumbled to his feet and discovered Bella lying spread-eagled on the beach. An elephant seal had rolled on to each hand. Jack pushed and pushed but could not move the tonnes of blubber.

"Hurry up will you. I'm dying here!" screamed Bella.

"I'm doing my best," pleaded Jack.

He had to wake the seals, but how? As he shook the seals, the blubber just wobbled like jelly, and there was no way that they could feel anything through all that fat. Then Jack had an idea, he tickled one of their noses. The nose twitched, the seal stirred briefly, then started to snore again. More continuous tickling of his elephant trunk was required. Suddenly, the snoring stopped and the seal let out a long, contented sigh and stretched his huge body of blubber. Bella was released from one elephant seal manacle. Jack repeated the same ritual with the other seal.

"Like, oh the stench!" cried Bella, not sounding the least bit grateful. "What revolting, disgusting creatures."

"Yes, it does smell, like, our boys' changing room at school," agreed Jack.

"Well, I do not know anything about a boys' changing room. All I know is that we need to get out of here. The smell is like making me dizzy."

"Not without the others. Actually, I think that their elephant trunks are quite cute," teased Jack.

"Will you stop winding each other up. I need some help here." These words came from behind them, just three sleeping seals away. It was Flo. They found her wedged between two seals. Together, they tickled noses and prised her out from below two semi-conscious seals.

"Thanks," said Flo, rubbing the pins and needles from her body. "Have you seen my little brother?"

They stopped to listen to see whether any other of the elephant seals were speaking English. Rising above the deep, sonorous snoring of seals was a shrill, high-pitched nasal whistling. They discovered Ben sleeping happily nestled up to one seal and using another as a soft, blubbery pillow.

Jack tickled Ben's nose and he awoke with a start. Startled, he rose on his elbows, and through sleep-befuddled eyes he turned his head frantically from side to side.

"Where am I?" asked Ben in a trembling voice.

"In an elephant seal colony, stupid! Where do you think we are?" said Bella, showing not a single ounce of sympathy.

Ben reached for Flo and buried his head under her armpit.

Suddenly, the rhythmical snoring was broken by a thunderous roar. Bodies of blubber across the colony stirred like a Mexican wave. There was another roar and they turned to see two massive male seals rushing at each other across the shingle beach. As they clashed, they rose up on their fins to a height of over two metres. Their tummies slammed together. The beach appeared to shake under the impact. They twisted, turned, gouged and bellowed. With sharp fangs bared, they bit into each other's necks. Blood sprayed. Enraged and driven by the sight of 30 expectant females, now all fully awake and spectators to this violent dawn duel, they fought on. Steam rose from their bodies and their mouths dripped with blood. The smaller of the two males shimmied one way and then the other like a professional boxer, before ducking down and sinking his teeth into the soft neck of his assailant. His victim frantically swayed from side to side, seeking release from the jaws of pain. The teeth remained locked, and blood poured down the neck and chest, staining the surf. With an agonised howl, the larger male turned his head determinedly away from the females and towards the sea. Sensing victory, the small male released his grip and watched as his defeated adversary headed down the shingle shore. He let out a trumpeting roar. Triumphant, he was now master of the beach and the colony of female seals.

The children stood hypnotised by this violent clash. They watched as the bloodied, vanquished rival stumbled into the sea. Lying in the surf nearby was the tattered and punctured wreck of their life raft, barely recognisable and chewed to bits by the jagged rocks. Jack broke their trance.

"This is no place to be. Let's get out of here."

"What about the rope? It might come in useful," suggested Flo. She clambered down the shingle beach and untied the blue, nylon rope. Jack looked on with dawning respect.

As Flo climbed back, she noticed some mussels clinging to the rocks. She called to the others, but her words were lost, drowned by the thundering surf and the grunts of the elephant seals. She cupped her hands around her mouth.

"MUSSELS…COME DOWN!" Flo shouted.

The others joined her.

"Great," congratulated Jack. "Let's collect as many as we can."

"You must be joking," said a disgusted Bella, screwing up her face and further turning up her already turned-up nose. "I won't touch them, let alone eat them!"

"Beggars can't be choosers," said Jack. "These might be our only food."

"I'm no beggar," replied Bella.

While Flo and Jack stuffed the mussels into their pockets, Ben was not so keen. Holding up one shell and looking at it closely, he asked, "Do they bite?"

Bella looked on, sulking.

The sun was struggling to make its presence felt through the low, grey clouds. In the gloom, and looking across the heaving bodies of the seal colony, they could just make out a trail of penguins waddling and zig-zagging their way up the cliff.

"Let's follow them," suggested Jack.

"First an albatross, and now a bunch of penguins. Like whatever next?" said Bella scornfully.

"The albatross showed us the way through those rocks. The seals saved us from freezing to death. So why not trust the penguins, or maybe you have a brighter idea?" said Jack.

For once, Bella was lost for words and 'likes'.

They left the noisy and restless seals, following the waddling penguins away from the beach and up a steep incline. On their short, stumpy legs and clawing at the rocks with their large, webbed feet, the penguins performed a comical 'To the right, to the left' dance with arms outstretched. Ben, now wide awake and

relieved to be leaving the sea and the intimidating seals, could not resist imitating them as they clambered up the hill. As he waddled up the hill, bottom waggling and arms outstretched, he started to sing again:

"Heigh-ho, heigh-ho
It's off to work we go
Got to make your troubles go
Well, you keep on singing all day long
Heigh-ho, heigh-ho, heigh-ho, heigh-ho."

"Oh, do be quiet! Don't you like realise the trouble we are in?" said Bella.

"Trouble, what trouble?" asked Ben, and continued to waddle and sing. Unlike Ben, Jack and Flo shared Bella's concern. It was now all about survival at the southernmost tip of the world. With no adults to protect and guide them, just themselves to pitch their wits against hostile weather and terrain, their situation had echoes of 'The Lord of the Flies' thought Jack, quietly, to himself.

As they ascended to the summit, they heard a cacophony of noise. Confused, the children stopped to listen.

"What a weird sound," said Flo, perplexed. "Sounds like a herd of braying donkeys."

"Yes, braying donkeys in a massive tumble drier," agreed Jack.

"Are you like off your rockers?" said Bella. "Am I the only sane person here?"

"I only said sounds like," said Flo, defiantly.

Ben had reached the top, and the others stopped arguing and climbed to join him to solve the mystery.

They were greeted by the sight of thousands of chatty Magellanic penguins going about their business – building nests, laying eggs and foraging for food across a grey, bare, pockmarked landscape that resembled the surface of the moon. With black backs, outer flippers and caps, and with white bellies, inner flippers and stripes, they presented a sea of black and white. Most distinctive of all was the white band running from each eyebrow down under the faces, giving the impression of a colony of smiling clowns. A far cry from the blubbery, bellowing seals. The smell, however, was no better – a heady mix of ammonia and sulphur. Standing just 60 cms high, the penguins were not afraid of the children, and carried on oblivious of these 1.5 metre giants.

"We could be the first humans to have ever set foot here," Jack pointed out. This thought made them feel very lonely but excited at the same time. Jack had always fancied himself as an explorer.

"I'm hungry," stated Ben, now bored of imitating the penguins.

"Let's have a look at the emergency kit," Jack replied hopefully. He unzipped the green pack. The others crowded around expectantly. Inside were the following survival items:

- A first aid kit
- Emergency rations, including ship's biscuits, dried fruit, multivitamin tablets, chocolate and a slab of Kendal Mint Cake
- Flares
- Compass
- Mirror
- Fishing kit
- Torch and batteries
- Matches
- Water pouches and cups
- Swiss Army penknife
- Lightweight waterproof ponchos
- A metal container for evaporating seawater

Bella snatched at the mirror. "I'll like look after that." She took one look at her reflection and stepped back, horrified. Staring back at her was a girl with messy, matted hair, a dirt-smudged face and poached egg eyes. The once scarlet, ironed shirt was creased and tattered and patterned with salt water tidemarks.

"Who needs like a mirror anyway?" She recoiled as she chucked it back to Jack.

"It could come in useful should we see a plane," pointed out Jack. "Catch the sun off it and the flash of light beams for miles."

"There is little chance of a plane, let alone the sun ever making an appearance in this like God-forsaken place," said Bella, staring at the monochrome sky.

"The ship would have put out a 'mayday' emergency call," said Jack reassuringly. "Help must be on its way."

"They will be looking out at sea, not in a penguin colony, silly," pointed out Bella, rudely.

Jack swallowed his words and bit his tongue.

"I'm hungry and thirsty," whined Ben again.

Flo passed him a pouch of water and pack of ship's biscuits. He ripped them open and stuffed one into his mouth. His face contorted in disgust.

"Yuck, they taste like sawdust. I want the chocolate instead."

"I want never gets," said Flo dismissively. "Wash them down with water."

They all tucked into the biscuits and drank the water at the same time. They felt like their mouths were cement mixers. The chocolate was put back for another even more desperate time.

"I could boil some eggs," suggested Flo. Jack and Bella stared at her in surprise, while Ben did not react. He was still concentrating on the disappearing chocolate. "I bet that penguin over there is sitting on an egg. She can always lay another." Flo continued to impress

Jack and here was an ally for their survival. Under that dreamy exterior, she was clearly practical and resourceful, qualities that they would need if they were going to survive in this inhospitable place.

Driven by hunger, Ben crouched down by a nesting penguin and poked her in the bottom. Her neck swivelled quickly and, staring defiantly, she hissed at Ben.

"Oh, come on, give us an egg," pleaded Ben.

As if in answer, the penguin shifted and raised her bottom.

Taking this as an invitation, Ben reached for an egg, only to nipped smartly on the nose.

"Ouch!" cried Ben, clutching his nose.

"What a proper little Dr Dolittle!" laughed Bella, derisively. "Do you really think she understands you?"

The penguin remained standing, hissing and flapping her flippers.

The egg wobbled.

"Did you see that?" cried Ben.

"See what?" replied Bella. "The penguin like beating you up?"

"It wobbled." Ben knelt down further. "Now listen..."

The children heard the faintest of tapping. A crack appeared and a tip of a tiny beak emerged, followed by a small, shiny head with eyes clamped shut. A sticky little creature uncrumpled itself from its shell, with clumsy feet and flapping flippers. The eyes opened, dazed and fuzzy, and, staring expectantly at its mother, it unlocked its beak to let out a plaintive cry. The mother was waggling her head around with pride and then she bowed down to nuzzle her chick affectionately. The baby looked beyond its mother and stared agog at the crowded, noisy colony. The children looked around and witnessed numerous chicks breaking and clambering out of their eggs.

The children searched for unattended nests and were rewarded with four eggs, about the size of a goose egg and the colour of white marble. Having gathered some kindling of moss, lichen and bits of nest, and some penguin poo on standby, Jack triumphantly took out the matches. This air of triumph did not last for long.

"Oh, dash it! They feel damp," said a crestfallen Jack.

"Now what are we like going to do?" said Bella, unhelpfully as usual.

"These stones look like flints," said Flo, reaching down to pick up a milky white stone streaked with grey. "At Brownies' camp, we lit fires by striking flints on steel."

"Great one, Einstein! Where're we going find steel in the middle of nowhere?" said Bella sarcastically.

"This might help," said Jack, staring down at his wrist. There sat his watch, given to him on his 14th birthday by his grandfather. The glass was misted, and the second hand had stopped. The time read 5.11, the exact time the life raft had somersaulted them into the surf.

The wrist watch was backed by steel, with the engraved initials, JSP (Jack Sterling Pask) and 12th September 1994. With a certain amount of reluctance and nostalgia, Jack unstrapped the watch. He took a flint, and while the others watched expectantly as he dragged the flint across the steel, Jack thought of his grandfather miles away back home alone in Kettering. Missing his wife and Jack's grandmother – a victim to cancer some three years ago.

Nothing happened, nothing but a scratched line across his initials. Jack tried again... nothing. What would his grandfather be thinking?

"Let me try," said Flo. Jack passed over his treasured watch. With a subtler, female touch, she drew the flint deftly across the steel. Up shot a spark, first hissing and then just as quickly fizzling out.

"A spark, a spark!" exclaimed Ben excitedly, thinking of his stomach. "Well done, sis."

Now kneeling down close to the small heap of moss

and lichen, Flo struck again. A spark flew, and the moss flared briefly, then dissolved from flame to smoke.

"Help me here, Ben," said Flo. "Blow on it gently when you see a flame. Jack, cup your hands around the moss to stop the wind." Bella looked on, shaking her head.

Flint to steel, cupping hands, flying spark, flaring moss and gentle blowing, the moss ignited. Throwing on lichen and twigs, the fire started to take.

"We did it, we did it!" cried Ben, dancing around excitedly.

They piled on pellets of penguin poo for good measure, and with the fire burning blue and smelly, it was not long before the eggs were dancing in the bubbling water.

"How long do you think we should cook them for?" inquired Flo, taking charge of the cooking.

"You know how I like mine. Nice and runny in the middle," ordered Ben.

"This is not a hotel and I am not taking orders," said Flo, rather peeved that Ben was claiming all the credit for the fire. "Don't you dare ask for soldiers. They are bigger than hen eggs, so let's try one after ten minutes. Can someone do the timing?"

As Jack's watch was now a firelighter, the others looked at their wrists. They then realised that they did not have a watch between them. After what seemed like ten minutes and 600 elephants later, Flo scooped one egg from the pan.

"I'm not having the first one," announced Ben suspiciously.

"Well, I'm not going to be like a guinea pig," added Bella.

Jack volunteered and he broke the egg. Transparent, gooey liquid specked with streaks of yellow seeped out.

"Yuck," said Ben.

Flo boiled them for much, much longer. Towards the end, she added the mussels.

The eggs sat in the pan surrounded by opened mussel shells.

"What a combination," said Jack. "Penguin eggs with a side order of mussels." Secretly, he was proud to be living off the proceeds of nature on their first day in the wilds.

They were like no eggs they had ever eaten before. Despite all the boiling, the 'white' of the egg had remained bluish, semi-translucent and jelly-like, but fortunately the yolk was a rich, yellow colour. The overwhelming taste and smell was one of salty fish, but it was not too overpowering, and in their hungered state they wolfed down the lot.

The mussels were not so popular. Bella stubbornly refused to touch one, and Ben thought they looked like a pile of snot. Flo and Jack polished off the lot. They congratulated themselves for living at one with nature, and they were so pleased that they treated themselves to a bit of chocolate each.

Chapter 4 – Cave of Hands

"We must keep moving. The sun is getting lower and we are very exposed out here. Let's look for some shelter before nightfall," said Jack, with a sense of urgency.

The others nodded their consent, and they shivered as a chill crept down their spines. Stuffing more eggs into the emergency pack, they headed off the only way they could – away from the sea, away from the company of thousands of chatty penguins and towards the steep, jagged granite mountains. The plain was desolate, barren and rocky. Battered by the winds and storms, no vegetation grew apart from the lichen clinging to the stones. The sky was turning a threatening gunmetal grey and a headwind was starting to pick up, forcing them to lean forward in order to make any progress at all. Flo took Ben's hand and had to drag him along. Horizontal rain stung their faces and the wet, rocky ground became treacherous and slippery. They soldiered on towards the mountains in search of respite from the biting wind. The light was fading quickly.

Out of the gloom loomed a herd of 12 guanacos. Heads bowed and ears pricked, they picked their way through the maze of rocks. They were walking in a procession one behind the other. Every so often, they switched the lead to share the burden of facing directly into the unforgiving wind and rain.

"They're streamlining," said Jack in awe. "I saw that once in the Tour de France." The others did not hear, as his words were snatched away by the relentless wind. The children followed, relieved to have some company. As they started to climb, the path narrowed and started to twist as the slope became steeper and steeper. While the guanacos were confident and surefooted, the children struggled to keep up, slipping, sliding and stumbling, increasingly worried that they would lose their footing and plunge headlong down the mountainside. Rocks and pebbles, loosened by the children, tumbled down the ravine.

Ever upwards they staggered, at times on all fours, seeking to stay on the thin, twisting ribbon of the path. Their fingers clawed at the rocks and their toes dug deep. Eventually, they reached a small, narrow ledge, and in the dusk they could just make out the yawning mouth of a cave. They followed the guanacos inside. There was not much space, but it was a welcome relief to be out of the howling wind and the lashing rain. They gently pushed their way through the guanacos and huddled down in a small hollow at the back. With the body heat of a dozen guanacos, it was not long before warmth returned to their bodies and they started to feel their fingers, feet and noses again.

In the darkness, Jack fumbled for the torch. It flickered on and they were stunned by what they saw. On the cave walls and roof were hundreds of hands –

stencilled human hands, large and small, all with fingers splayed. They were in different colours – reds, purples, yellows, blacks and whites.

"Wow," said Ben in awe. "It's like a cartoon strip." Amongst the hands, he pointed out human stick figures armed with spears stalking four-legged, horse-like beasts. "They look like the animals we are sharing the cave with."

"It means that we are not alone," pointed out Jack. "All we have seen so far is animals. Now we know that humans have survived here before us."

"Very reassuring!" muttered Bella sarcastically, pouring water on Jack's optimism. "Why they'd want to live in this God-forsaken place escapes me. And why'd you want to spend your time leaving handprints in a cave? Desperate boredom, probably."

"This is where they would have lived," said Flo. "It's rock art to make them feel at home."

"Some home – like cold, damp, dark, and what's worse is we're having to share it with a bunch of smelly animals that look like a bunch of small camels," Bella continued to whinge.

"They saved us from the storm," pointed out Jack. "And without them we'd be freezing to death."

The children settled down on damp beds of rock and miraculously, exhausted by the day's adventures – shipwreck, elephant seals, penguin eggs and guanacos, they fell into a deep sleep.

Jack was awoken by a rumbling tummy of egg and mussels and a pain in his back. The other children still slept, and the guanacos were gently snoring, resting their heads on each other's bottoms. He switched on the torch and discovered a sharp, curved claw about 15 cms long. '*So this was what had been poking him in the back,* Jack thought, *and clearly the guanacos were not the only animals to seek shelter in the cave.*' With a shiver running down his spine, he tucked the claw in his pocket and tiptoed his way through the animals. He stepped out into the night. The sky was lit up with thousands of stars. Never in his life had he seen so many stars. The moon was a perfect crescent and the milky way sent streaks of light across the sky towards the southern cross. It was strange to see Orion upside down with sword pointing upwards. He could not see the Big Dipper anywhere. Suddenly, two shooting stars shot across the sky, leaving glittering trails in their wake. *'That has to be a good omen,'* thought Jack. *'Perhaps we might, just might find our way out of Patagonia.'* Jack returned to his rocky bed.

The children awoke to a magical and bizarre scene. The sun beamed through the entrance to the cave, casting dappled guanaco shadows across the sea of hands. They had to pinch themselves to realise where they were and the reality of their situation – they had survived their first night stranded at the bottom of the world with no adults. The guanacos were getting ready to leave. They were shaking out their legs, stretching their necks and rolling their shoulders. The children did the same.

"I would kill to have their like eyelashes and lips," said Bella. Flo sniggered and the boys looked at her in amazement. "Just look at those long, curled lashes and pouted lips."

"Make your mind up! You just called them smelly animals," said an exasperated Jack. "Bet you don't want their buck teeth and pointed ears."

"I'd like their dark, soulful eyes," chirped up Flo.

"I dig their fawn fur and snow white underbellies," said Ben. "Great for keeping me warm."

"Hate to break up this guanaco appreciation society," said Jack. "Look what I slept on last night." He reached in his pocket and drew out the claw, the length of his hand. The others gasped.

"Now that is the claw of a very big animal!" exclaimed Flo.

"Better get out of here!" cried Ben. "What happens if it comes back for it?"

"Claws like grow again, silly," replied Bella.

Driven by curiosity, the children returned somewhat nervously to the place they had slept. Lying on the cave floor were scraps of leathery skin covered with stiff, slightly wavy, reddish hair. The skin was surrounded by brown, knobby pellets about the size of a cricket ball.

"Oh goodness, this skin looks fresh," said Jack, holding up a piece up for close inspection.

"And I think you'll find those balls are poo," said Flo.

"Must be a monster to have poo that big," chipped in Ben.

"Oh great," said Bella, sarcastically. "Our first night with a bunch of smelly elephant seals followed by a night sleeping in a monster's bed. Just my luck!"

"I'm taking these back home for identification," said Jack excitedly. "We could have discovered an animal unknown to man."

"In your like dreams," said Bella. Jack ignored her as he tucked a dung ball and piece of skin in his pocket to join the claw. The mere mention of 'home' had cast a shadow over the children.

"We must get moving," urged Jack.

As they jostled their way through the herd, they pushed past a matronly female. Hiding behind her was her baby.

"Gosh, how cute," said Ben, and he reached out to pat the soft, downy fur of the baby. Her protective mother hissed, rolled her tongue and pursed her lips. Instinct told Ben to duck, and just in time. A globule of spit shot over his head and slammed against one of the painted hands on the wall.

"Wow, impressive – that is some weapon," said Ben, looking at the mother in awe. As the protective guanaco was preparing for another shot, Flo quickly took Ben's hand and led him away from the baby.

"Let's follow them," said Jack.

"No like way. They spit," said Bella in disgust, quickly forgetting their gorgeous eyelashes.

"Just stay away from the baby," advised Flo.

The weather was in stark contrast to yesterday. A gentle breeze caressed their faces, and the high cumulus clouds billowed up against the azure sky. For the first time, they could feel the warmth of the sun.

Following the guanacos, they traversed the steep scree slope. Upwards, ever upwards, towards the granite peaks as jagged as shark teeth. Away from the sea and further into this mysterious land. The rocks were now sprinkled with snow and ice and now high above sea mist clinging to the coast. They squeezed their way through two granite teeth. Nothing in their experience had prepared them for the sight that greeted their eyes. The children stood bewitched.

Chapter 5 – Crossing the Glacier

A massive glacier, resembling a vast expanse of cloud, appeared below them. The ice, streaked with areas of dazzling steely-blue, glistened a brilliant white in the sunlight. From high up in the mountains, the glacier unfurled and rasped its way down the valley floor, sweeping all before it. It ended eventually in a tottering cliff of ice, hovering precariously above milky, turquoise waters. A thundering, echoing boom made the children jump as a huge slab of ice crashed into the waters, sending a tsunami of waves down the icy river. This truly was another world beyond their wildest imagination.

"We must keep going north so our only choice is to cross it," said Jack, breaking the spell and echoing what they were all thinking. "There looks to be no way around."

As if answer, the guanacos suddenly took fright and danced off down the hillside away from the booming glacier. The mother was the last to leave. Once the baby was a safe distance away, the mother turned towards the children and looked them in the eye as if to say, *Now you are on your own,* before skipping off after the others.

Patagonia was now a very lonely and frightening place. They scrambled down the rocky valley side to the very edge of the glacier. The sun was low in the sky. From above, the glacier had appeared relatively smooth. Up close, it was contorted, convulsed, and creased. Pockets of vivid blue hinted at treacherous crevasses.

"We better camp here overnight," suggested Jack. "There's not much light left, and the last thing we want to do is to be stranded on the glacier in the dark."

"What do you mean 'camp'?" complained Bella. "We have like *nothing* to camp with."

It was indeed a barren landscape. As the sun dropped below the hills, casting the valley into shade, strange figures started to emerge from the ground. Patagonian Mara, with pointed, hare-like ears, a body resembling a small deer and back legs longer than the front, they were extraordinary-looking animals. Their fur was a brownish grey, but their bottoms were a darker shade and fringed by a white band; their bellies were the colour of snow. They were the size of a Labrador that you would find at home. Giving the children not even a casual glance, the young romped, oblivious to their presence. Playing hide and seek amongst the burrows while the adults looked on indulgently.

"The animals here get weirder and weirder," said Ben. Two young babies jumped over his feet as they chased each other.

"So far the animals have always helped us," pointed out Jack.

"I can't like see these strange-looking animals helping us," said Bella.

"Look at their burrows," said Flo, "it'll be a squeeze, but there is enough room for us to shelter for the night." Jack was becoming increasingly impressed with her resourcefulness.

The Maras looked on placidly as four families were kicked out of their burrows. They were not homeless for long, as they were soon taken in by their neighbours. The children settled down contentedly in their burrows, snug as bugs in rugs. However, they would not sleep for long...

First, they all awoke to Ben screaming. He was sitting bolt upright, pointing with a trembling finger and staring wide-eyed at the far corner of the burrow.

"Two huge eyes," he stammered. "Two huge eyes just staring at me."

They all looked and sure enough there were two eyes – two coal black pupils fringed by a vivid yellow.

Certainly, they were not the eyes of a Patagonia Mara. As they stared, amazed, the eyes blinked. Jack grabbed the torch. In the beam, an owl was revealed.

"Whatever next - an owl that lives underground!" said Jack incredulously.

"I suppose he'd struggle to find like a tree around here," said Bella, matter-of-factly.

They returned to their burrows, and Ben fell asleep strangely reassured that he was sharing his burrow with an owl.

The glacier was a living beast and was in a particularly angry mood that night. It groaned, roared and thundered as it pushed, swept, carved and advanced its way down the valley floor. Huge rocks were cast aside as simply as chucking toys out of a pram. Every so often, a resounding crash would pierce the night as yet another massive slab of ice would belly flop into the turquoise waters. This was not a place for a peaceful night's sleep.

At first light, the children emerged bleary-eyed from their burrows. The valley was still cast in shadow, and there was a sharp chill in the air. They shivered, not just from the cold but also from the sight of the monstrous glacier, which they were set to cross that day. They shared the same thoughts. *'How were they going to find their way across this volatile, powerful beast?'* The ice was – all pinnacles, folds and crevasses. It was a maze to beat all mazes. A treacherous maze that stretched for miles across to the other side of the valley. Nothing could possibly live on this flexing, freezing beast.

With a fire fuelled by Mara poo pellets, they boiled up the remaining penguin eggs to give them the energy for the challenge ahead. They picked out a distinctive crag shaped like a lion's head on the far side of the glacier. This would be their guide. Tentatively, they took their first steps on the ice.

The ice was brittle, fragile and noisy underneath their feet. Pinnacles of contorted ice rose three metres above their heads, obscuring their view and forcing them to take a twisting, turning path across. Soon they felt disorientated, and they could not be sure that they were not walking around in circles.

"It's a maze of ice," said Jack, echoing the thoughts of the others.

"Give me Hampton Court anytime," said Flo dreamily.

"Oh yes, that's where you can cheat by nipping through the hedges," pointed out Ben.

"Not like helpful," said Bella impatiently. "We need to stop faffing around. In this cold, I'm losing the will to live."

"At Hampton Court, you have bridges and lookouts to help you find your way out," said Jack.

"That's more like it," replied Bella. "Why don't you climb up and see? Flo will give you a leg up." She was always volunteering others when she the thought the job was beneath her.

"Easier said than done," said Jack, inspecting the ice. "It's rock hard."

"Try hacking away with the knife," suggested Flo. "You could cut some footholds."

Jack hacked away and, eventually, he had cut a path up the three metre wall of ice. He failed in his first three attempts. He lost his footing and slid back down to the bottom. Encouragingly, each time he tried he got higher. On his fourth attempt, he reached the top.

"Come on then, what can you see?" demanded Bella, impatient as ever.

"A sea of ice," replied Jack.

"Can you see the lion's head?" asked Flo.

"What the hell are you talking about a lion's head for?" blurted out Bella without thinking.

"The rock on the other side, stupid!" said Ben rudely, staring up at Bella and pointing and twisting his finger against the side of his head. Jack and Flo could not suppress a giggle. For Bella, this was the ultimate embarrassment being put in her place by an eight-year-old.

Bella was relieved when Jack broke the silence.

"No lion's head. No nothing. Ice, ice, ice..."

As Jack slid down the ice wall, the children felt a sense of imprisonment. Which way to turn now – right, left, forward, or worse still behind them? It was anybody's guess. While climbing, Jack had kept moving, but the others had been stationary and were getting colder and colder.

"We must keep moving. I'm not going to lie, I'm chilled to the bone," urged Flo, ever practical and sensible. A welcome contrast to Bella, who clearly was not a team player and had a habit of speaking before thinking.

They squeezed through a gap to the right. Unusually, the sky was a brilliant blue and the sun beamed down fiercely. The reflection off the ice was dazzling. The children squinted their way through the shimmering, white maze. Occasionally, the white would be punctuated by a vivid blue – a sign of dangerous crevasses lurking underneath. They gingerly tiptoed their way around these mantraps. Despite the sun, the cold was starting to take a grip on them. They had all but lost sensation in their feet, and their fingers were turning blue. Ben was starting to shiver and blink uncontrollably.

"I'm starting to see white spots. It's like I'm in a snow storm," said Ben in panic. "Everything's becoming so blurred." Frantically, he rubbed his eyes and shook his head. "It's no good, it's getting worse."

"It could be snow blindness," suggested Jack. "I got it when I was skiing without goggles."

"I can't see!" The other children turned to see Ben sleep walk his way into an ice wall and collapse to the ground.

Just as Flo was reaching down to haul him back to his feet, a black shadow swept across Ben's prone body. She glanced up to see what was circling above their heads A lone, black vulture – an Andean condor. Gliding downwards in ever-decreasing circles, they started to make out his distinctive white collar, sharp, hooked beak, knife-like claws and ruddy face. Far from feeling threatened by this sign of impending death, the children's spirits lifted as they were no longer alone. In their own different ways, the animals and birds they

had encountered so far had all helped them to survive. The children were starting to share the same thoughts. *'Who could know how to cope with this hostile land better than they? Could this condor, like the albatross before him, show them the way out of this maze of ice?'*

The condor landed with a splash of feathers just above their heads, claws digging into the ice to stay on his precarious perch. His red eyes looked down at them. He certainly did not look like he was eyeing them up as his next dinner. Far from being scared, the children felt hope sweep through them. With a knowing look, he spread his wings and glided upwards.

They followed him. At first, Flo led Ben by the hand, issuing instructions along the way – right, left, mind the gap, bump ahead. It was a slow, twisting and crooked path through the ice and across and around crevasses.

"It's too dangerous," said Jack. "One wrong step and Ben will fall down a crevasse, and we will have with no chance of saving him."

He unravelled the nylon rope from around his neck. Deftly, he tied the rope around Ben's waist, before attaching it to himself. The condor waited patiently. Stumbling, slipping and sliding, the children struggled to keep up with the weaving path of the condor. The cold was now seeping deep into their bodies. Numbed by this freezing cold, their movements were now clumsy and erratic. With a blind Ben, progress was even slower. It was a race against time to escape this maze of ice.

Suddenly, the sea of ice started to break up. First, a glimpse of a grey granite rock, and then the rocky side of the valley rose above them.

"Look! There's the lion's head," cried Jack excitedly. The condor landed on this rocky crag and watched them as they stumbled and collapsed onto the firm ground.

"Thank you," said Flo breathlessly, as she led Ben gently to a rock to sit down on. With a nod of his collared head, the majestic condor soared high into the mountains.

Thankfully, the sky was still blue, and basking in the sunshine it was not long before their freezing bones started to thaw. They slept the sleep of angels, blissfully unaware of the occasional groan and rumble of the glacier.

Ben was the first to stir, jolted awake by a nightmare

that he had gone blind. He opened his eyes to darkness. He screamed and started frantically to rub his eyes. Opening his eyes again, there were specks of colour floating around like confetti. More rubbing, and this time a ghostly shadow loomed above him. Like a developing photo in a darkroom, the concerned and kind face of his sister emerged.

"I can see again!" echoed through the valley and drowned out the grumbling glacier.

Chapter 6 - Rhubarb Forest

"Let's get moving," urged Jack, "I don't fancy another freezing night beside this noisy monster of a glacier."

Reluctantly, the children shook out their stiff, aching limbs, but they did not need much encouragement to turn their backs on the glacier that had so nearly claimed their lives.

"I reckon we have another two hours of daylight," said Jack, as they traversed down the steep valley side, picking their way across the stony slope. Moving ever downwards, they could feel the air getting noticeably warmer, and the sun still shone valiantly in the sky, chasing away the wispy clouds. Small bushes started to appear, at first solitary and sparse, but gradually thickening as they descended. These spindly, hardy shrubs then gave way to box-leafed calafate bushes bejewelled in bright red berries.

"Do you think we can eat them?" asked an excited Ben. "I'm starving."

"They do look like redcurrants," replied Flo.

"That's good enough for me," said Ben, tentatively popping one berry into his mouth, unwilling to wait for any further debate.

The others watched with bated breath, half expecting him to spit it out. Suddenly, a smile lit up Ben's face.

"They taste like blueberries."

"Don't be like so ridiculous," scoffed Bella, in her characteristically dismissive manner.
"Your loss," said Ben, stuffing a handful in his mouth. Jack and Flo followed suit, while Bella looked on shaking her head. Even a collective "Yum..." could not persuade her. They filled their pockets and the emergency pack with red berries.

The trees that they had seen in Patagonia started to appear. At first, they were tentative and spindly, bent double and clinging on for dear life to unforgiving rocky earth against the ravishes of the prevailing wind. Descending further, they found themselves in a copse of miniature beech trees. It looked as if a Japanese bonsai enthusiast had been let loose in the wood. Venturing down further, they found themselves in a gnarly, old man forest – skeletal trunks and twisted branches. These trees were covered in white and orange mushrooms. They stopped to pick them, more to wind up Bella than with any intention to eat them.

The forest kept getting thicker and thicker, darker and darker. Until now, the birds had gone on chattering as if they were alone on earth. But not here. One by one, the birds stopped their singing, and nothing was moving, either in the leaves or on the ground. The forest became utterly and eerily silent. Their breathing was the only sound they could hear.

Warily, the children looked behind them. They could no longer see their path; it had closed in on them.

"We better mark our way back," muttered Jack, breaking the silence. His voice was tense and tremulous.

Flo's shirt was ripped and she pulled out a mass of threads to leave a gaping hole. These threads she now tied around the branches as they pushed their way through. Bamboo now barred their way and, thirty minutes on, they were becoming desperate and scared. The forest surrounded them, tightening its hold and eating up the space. It was now too dense for animals. *'Not even a fox could find its way through this stuff,'* thought Flo to herself. The forest was becoming impenetrable and suffocating. They looked up, searching in vain for a glimpse of the failing sunlight. The foliage was closing in, squeezing, enveloping and stifling, and they were shrouded by spider webs. They parted the flailing creepers only for them to clamp shut like Venus flytraps, grabbing at their ankles, legs and arms. They felt an overwhelming sense of claustrophobia. Ben started to whine like a lost puppy.

They fought and struggled on, only to hit a wall of thorny, reddish-coloured stalks rising two metres above their heads. They looked up to see a canopy of heart-shaped, wavy leaves the size of a man.

"Looks just like giant rhubarb," said Flo amazed. "Truly this is place of giants."

They cut their way through the stalks to emerge blinking into a clearing surrounded by giant rhubarb.

Exhausted, they dropped to the ground, gulping in the sweet, rhubarb-scented air. They could think of no better place to camp. They bent the stalks and interlocked the heart-shaped leaves to create an umbrella above their heads. They gorged themselves on sweet

berries, and despite their initial concerns, they ate the white and orange mushrooms – they had the taste and texture of earthy bread. Driven by hunger, even Bella nervously nibbled away and washed the mushrooms down with water from a nearby stream. They even experimented with boiling up the rhubarb stems for dessert – it did seem odd to be cooking their accommodation! The result was disappointing. The rhubarb was tart and stringy, and they spent the rest of the evening picking out the fibres from their teeth. They did not have a toothbrush between all four of them.

Inside their rhubarb shelter, they felt warm for the first time in the last three days.

"What's like the plan?" asked Bella, still chewing nervously at a mushroom.

"We have to keep going north," replied Jack. "That's where we will find people. A village, maybe."

"I'm enjoying being without adults telling me what to do, always on my back," said Ben.

Bella raised an eyebrow and chose to ignore Ben." But which way is north? How do we know which way to go?" she enquired.

"At night we have the southern cross, and during the day we have sunrise and sunset," replied Jack.

"But we need a cloudless sky and we have seen precious little of that," said Bella.

"There must be a compass in the emergency kit," said Flo.

"I didn't see one," said Jack, rummaging through the pack, but sure enough, nestling in a side pocket, was a compass. "Eureka!"

"What about the search party? Surely your parents would have raised the alarm? It can't be long before they find us," said Bella, clutching at straws.

"Surely you mean our parents, not your parents," replied Jack.

"My Dad will be too busy to notice, always like working, working, working," said Bella bitterly. "As for Mum, she is probably sunning herself at the tennis club. They sent me off to boarding school at the first opportunity."

"Do you have any brothers or sisters?" asked Flo.

"I'm an only child, all alone in the world," replied Bella sadly. "Never more so than now."

While Ben fidgeted awkwardly, it dawned on Jack and Flo that underneath the prickliness and bluster, there was a sad and vulnerable young girl. If they were going to survive, they needed to survive together as a team. Understanding, tolerating and supporting each other was the key to their survival.

Moving on, Jack said, "It's hard to face reality, but our parents probably believe we went down with the ship. Even if they find the life raft, you saw it, in all likelihood they will think we drowned."

"Yes, our survival was indeed a miracle," said Flo.

"So you're saying there is nobody...like coming out to save us," said Bella.

"Yes, but we do have each other," replied Jack.

"And the animals and birds," chirped Flo. "They have helped us to survive so far."

Lying on the warm, soft, peaty floor, they had hoped for the sleep of angels. Instead, they slept fitfully. The rush of wings of the night birds, their squawks and cries; the furtive scampering of little mammals; thousands of rustling sounds and the dull clamour of nocturnal creatures – insects, mice, raptors and hunters. As the night was ending, it fell quiet, and the sounds faded.

Chapter 7- River Tightrope

They were awoken by a silence so heavy that it seeped into their ears. Shafts of light now peeped through the rhubarb leaves. Despite the disturbed night, they felt refreshed by the warmth - no more shivering and stiff limbs. After breakfasting on just berries and mushrooms (unfortunately the remaining penguin eggs had broken while they stumbled their way across the glacier), they were lured by the sound of flowing water. They emerged, blinking, out of the rhubarb and on to the banks of a river. Just to their right lay a large pool of blue-green water, fed from above by a cascading waterfall over 30 metres high. At the top, filling the groove in the rocks, was a hanging glacier.

Oblivious, Ben ripped off his clothes and ran naked across the rocks to the edge of pool. Before Flo could warn her brother, he dived in head first, with a shriek of excitement. Ben felt like a fist had grabbed his heart, and the air was forced out of his lungs as he broke the icy surface. He let out an agonised yell and thrashed his head from side to side and then, with frantic strokes, he headed as quickly as possible to the rocks. Shaking, he belly flopped out of the water, jumped to his feet and naked he danced like a crazed disco dancer.

"Freeeeee...zing," he yelped, with gritted teeth.

Laughter filled the air, and it came from an unexpected source – it was Bella.

They all bathed in the icy pool, scooping the water over their bodies, pleased to at last rub off the salt from the sea. They also washed their clothes and hung them on the rhubarb leaves to dry in the sunshine. Jack felt his tummy rumble and it was then that he remembered the fishing line in the emergency kit.

"Anybody fancy a spot of fishing?" he asked. Flo found a wiggly worm under a rock and they excitedly headed downstream in search of more tranquil and clear water. After five minutes clambering over rocks, Bella was stopped in her tracks by a flash of blue off to her right. She spied a kingfisher, dressed in unmistakeable vivid blue and orange plumage, now sitting on an overhanging branch.

"Where there is a kingfisher, there are fish," Bella pointed out. The others looked at her in amazement, as this was the first time she had said something constructive, rather than whinging the whole time.

"The birds and animals are at it again," smiled Flo.

Jack started to unravel the line and deftly squeezed the wiggly worm onto the hook.

"Let me do it," said Ben excitedly, grabbing for the line.

"No, Ben, wait and see how it is done," said Flo.

"I used to fish for trout with my dad in Devon," explained Jack. "The trick is to run the line and hook downstream. I reckon the fish are lying in that pool of still water under the kingfisher. They like quiet, shady water."

Jack chucked the line into the fast-flowing water only for it to be swept away downstream, missing the pool.

"I need to throw the line further across," said Jack, giving a running commentary.

With the others watching expectantly, this time the hook was swept into the pool. Jack tugged at the line three times and then started to reel it in again.

"Can't you be more like patient?" said Bella.

"The hook needs to keep moving or fish become suspicious," explained Jack. He tried again, nothing... and again, nothing – not the mere ripple of activity. The children looked crestfallen, while the kingfisher looked on quizzically, in no way intimidated by their presence. Were they the first humans he had ever seen?

"I have an idea," said Jack, scrambling around on the edge of the trees. He rose, holding up a plump stick. "This will act as a float." He tied the stick to the line about 30 cms above the hook. Again, he threw the line as far as he could across the river, and again it meandered out into the pool. Now the hook did not immediately drop to the bottom and he could leave it there for longer while still tugging on the line. Driven by hunger, the children's eyes bored into the shady depths willing the fish, if there were any fish, to be tempted.

A flash of darting silver, a slight ripple on the surface – were their eyes deceiving them? Did the stick sink just for a split second? Suddenly, the float dropped downwards and Jack tugged on the line. It bobbed back to the surface and the children let out a collective sigh of disappointment. Jack pulled in the line again and the worm had disappeared.

"Clever, canny fish," commented Jack. "At least we know there are fish." Flo already had a worm waiting and he carefully threaded it onto the hook while Bella grimaced.

The line again floated into the pool. More tugging, more watching, more waiting... then suddenly, the float dropped like a stone, quicker this time. Jack pulled on the line. The line stayed taut and started to weave and dart across the surface.

"We've hooked one!" shouted Ben, jumping around excitedly. Flo and Bella danced around, while Jack reeled in a writhing fish 30 cms long. Long, skinny and stripy, the fish sported an olive green top with a pinkish band running across its middle, fading to a silver underbelly and a pearl white bottom. Its body was also adorned in black spots.

"A rainbow trout," said Jack, unhooking the fish, "they are great to eat."

"It's almost too beautiful to eat," replied Bella.

"Oh, come on," said Jack.

"I did say like '*almost*'", said Bella, with a wry smile.

"Can I have a go?" asked Ben eagerly. They all had a go. Even Bella was animated by the experience and jumped and shrieked as she reeled one in.

"That's the first fish I have ever caught," she stated proudly.

Finally, with seven trout lying on the bank, Flo said, "Let's leave some for our kingfisher."

They cooked a delicious early lunch of trout and mushroom, and for the first time in three days their stomachs stopped rumbling. They ate one each, and they filleted the remaining three, leaving them to dry in the sun

"I almost feel normal again," said Jack, patting his stomach.

Refreshed, they all knew that they had to keep moving.

"Which way is north?" asked Flo.

"Let me guess, it's that direction," said Bella, pointing across the river. Jack pulled out the compass. The needle quivered and then settled, pointing unerring across the river.

"Typical," said Bella, with a shrug and a sigh.

"Well, we know that upstream is no good," said Jack, "there's no way we can climb that waterfall. Let's have a search downstream."

For over an hour clambering across rocks, the river failed to narrow and the current remained torrential.

After the excitement of the fishing, the reality was starting to sink in again.

"What exactly are we looking for?" asked an exasperated Bella. "A bridge? Fat chance of that happening. At this rate, we will end up back at the sea with those smelly seals and noisy penguins."

"We need to keep believing," said Flo.

Onwards they stumbled and the journey was tough. At times, they had to wade through the icy waters, clinging to the rocks to make sure they did not lose their footing, and at other times, they had to climb over huge boulders. Occasionally, they fought their way through the thick vegetation and trees lining the river banks.

They could hear a distant roar. Louder and louder it became as they struggled their way along the river bank.

"What's that?" asked Ben, puzzled.

"It's probably like an angry, hungry pride of lions," teased Bella.

"A what?" cried Ben.

"Don't worry, little bro. It's just Bella teasing you," said Flo. "There are no lions in the Americas. I think you'll find it's a waterfall."

Ben looked Bella straight in the eye and stuck out his tongue. Bella looked like she had just sucked a lemon.

They soon discovered that Flo was right. Suddenly, the trees and dense vegetation vanished to be replaced by sky. The river had also disappeared. It was now plunging and cascading down a 40 metre vertical drop. At any other time, this would be a magnificent, breath-taking sight – a sight that would attract thousands of tourists and a mecca for photographers. Rainbows flickered across the plumes of spray, the water boiled and thundered, and swifts darted in and out of the falls. Virgin forest stretched out below them towards the horizon split by the silvery ribbon of the river.

"This is beautiful," said Flo, dreamily.

"Truly spectacular," agreed Jack. "Do you think we are the first people to see these falls?"

"Let's quit all the lovey-dovey stuff," retorted Bella. "How the hell are we going to climb down there?"

"Language," said Ben, dramatically putting his hands over his ears. Now it was Bella's turn to stick out her tongue.

"Well, we can't go back," Jack pointed out.

"That's like vertical," said Bella, in a quivering voice.

"Where there's a will, there's a way," replied Jack.

"That's so crass," said Bella. "I might have vertigo."

"*Might* being the operative word," interjected Flo, under her breath.

"Come on... this is getting us nowhere," said Jack. "We know that upstream is no good, so we must go down. I'll lead and we'll go slowly. Just don't look down."

Choosing the route as far away as possible from the wet, slippery rocks and the spray of the cascading water, Jack lowered himself tentatively over the edge, his feet searching for footholds amongst the rocks and tree roots. Ben went next, followed by Bella and Flo. Progress was slow. Toes dug in, fingers clenched, chests pressed against the rocks, they edged their way down. Their hearts hammered and their breathing came out in erratic, short pants. Jack's words echoed in their heads, *'Don't look down'*. Slowly and steadily, they made it to the bottom of the waterfall. While the others were greatly relieved, Bella was obsessing over the state of her fingernails.

Ignoring the inviting and beautiful pool, they pressed on downstream, leaving the roar of the falls behind. The going was again challenging and, after an hour, they were on the verge of giving up hope. Suddenly, emerging out of the foliage, they saw a tree that had miraculously fallen over the river.

"There's our bridge," announced Jack, triumphantly. "Any volunteers for going first?" Silence...

"I'll go," piped Ben. "Remember, sis, we had such a bridge close to our house in England. I crossed it heaps of times."

"That's brave, Ben," said Jack, "but you must go with this rope around your waist. Remember not to look down."

Flo gave her brother a big, reassuring hug. Ben climbed on the trunk and slowly edged across. At first, he could leapfrog on his bottom.

"Gosh, this is a piece of cake," said Ben, turning to face them. "Look! No hands!"

"Ben!" screamed Flo, "Don't be so stupid."

"What a show off," said Bella, under her breath.

Halfway across, Ben was forced to stand up to push past some awkward branches. The rope kept getting caught and he had to give it a tug to free himself. Jack watched intently, as he was Ben's anchor on the bank. Ben had fallen silent and his face was screwed up in concentration as he weaved his way through the branches. He reached one particular protruding limb, clinging on as he leaned out to ease himself around it. It was then that he made the mistake of looking down. He turned pale and his legs started to shake violently.

"I can't do this," said Ben trembling.

Flo shouted, "Just hang..."

'Snap!' the branch splintered and Ben fell backwards

with a yell into the icy torrent. With an almighty splash, he disappeared. Jack braced himself, jamming his legs against rocks and taking the strain. The rope held. 20 metres downstream, Ben's head popped up, coughing and spluttering. Then, with arms flailing and flapping, he started to bodysurf the white water. Hand over hand, Jack gradually hauled Ben to the bank. Shaking and shocked, he lay exhausted on the rocks.

In a faint voice, Ben said, "Now I know what it is like to be one of those trout."

"I'll go," piped up Bella. The others turned in amazement. "My mum forced me to do ballet at school. I hated it, but it was good for my balance."

"Are you sure?" said Jack.

"Hurry up and tie that rope around my waist before I change my mind."

Bella edged tentatively across. She made it to the once protruding and now broken branch where Ben had fallen. Step by step, metre by metre, she got closer and closer to the opposite bank. She fought her way through the tree's limbs, reaching out like fingers intent on pushing her off. Agile and poised, she moved and then, with an exuberant jump, she sprung down.

"I made it!" danced Bella. It was the first time the others had seen her so animated and excited.

Bella untied the rope, and Jack dragged it back across the fast-flowing river.

"You go next," he said to Flo. Slowly, Flo edged her way across. It was Ben's turn next; he had just about recovered from his first attempt and, with cries of encouragement, he reached the other bank. Flo and Bella, working together as a team, prepared themselves as anchors, while Jack double checked the knot around his waist. Jack clambered up on the trunk and, with measured step, he joined them on the other side.

Chapter 8 - Monkey Puzzle Island

There was no time for celebration, as it was now well into the afternoon. They ventured northwards, following the compass through the thick tangle of trees. It was dark and humid, and progress was tortuously slow. The air hummed with insects.

"Look, it seems to be getting lighter up ahead," said Jack encouragingly. Shafts of sunlight were breaking through the forest canopy and, within minutes, they stepped out, blinking, into an apocalyptic scene. The forest suddenly gave way to an arid and desolate landscape. A river of black lava swept down the hillside. Trees lay mauled, smothered and suffocated, and no vegetation grew. High above to their left, a volcano smoked ominously.

"Don't like tell me that way is north," said Bella, pointing across the lava field. The compass could not lie. "What is it with this place – one minute we are crossing like a freezing glacier, and the next we have to contend with a lava field."

The lava was hard, rough and crusted below their feet, and it seemed to radiating heat. As they walked, plumes of ash flew up into their faces, causing them to choke and fight for breath. They raised their shirts to cover their mouths. They stumbled on and then, through the swirling ash, the faint shapes of giant evergreen pyramids started to gradually emerge.

"It is mirage?" Jack asked, confused.

They quickened their pace, and it was not long before they walked into an oasis of monkey puzzle trees. They were 20 towering, green parasols, branches spiralling and splaying in all directions and their leaves looking like the teeth of a hedge cutter. The air was fresh and clean, and green parakeets chatted amongst the branches. The ground was green and soft below their feet.

"I can think of no better place to spend the night," said Flo.

"What like weird trees are these?" asked Bella.

"They're monkey puzzle trees," replied Flo.

"And an even weirder name."

"Just look up," said Flo, "even a monkey cannot work out how to climb these trees." Rising above them was a chaos of branches shooting out at different angles, and you certainly could not imagine monkeys swinging from limb to limb.

"It is like we are on an island," said Jack. Surrounding them on all sides was the black, ominous lava. Just up the slope stood a huge boulder standing guard of these strange trees. Clearly this had stemmed and split the flow of the lava as it had swept down the hill, creating this oasis of life and beauty. Something dropped from above and thudded on the ground, narrowly missing Ben. He picked it up, and discovered that he was holding a large, oval seed pod.

"I wonder if you could eat it?" asked Ben, as ever thinking about his tummy. He handed the pod to Jack, and with a knife Jack cut through the tough, scaly skin to reveal a soft, pulpy inside protecting the seeds. He sliced up the yellow pulp and tentatively took a bite. The other children waited expectantly.

"It tastes like liquorice," proclaimed Jack with a smile.

"Great news, I love liquorice," said Ben. "Come on, Jack, hoist me up on your shoulders and I will pick some more."

"Don't worry about me, I hate the stuff," said Bella. "Most disgusting sweet ever."

"Then more for us," said Ben, as he reached up from Jack's shoulders.

Supper was indeed an odd combination – fillets of trout accompanied by liquorice-flavoured pod pulp.

"It is hard to believe that only this morning, we were fishing," said Flo. "Now we are on a monkey puzzle island surrounded by a lava field. Patagonia really is a very weird and strange place."

"I love the fact that when we wake up in the morning," said Jack, "we don't know what is going to happen or where we're going to end up. I find it invigorating – such a pleasant change from the routine of school and home."

"Yes, this is like a place of expecting the unexpected. I feel that it is casting a spell on me," said Bella with a faint smile. The other children looked at her in surprise – they certainly were not expecting her to say that.

Sheltered by the monkey puzzle trees and once the parakeets had gone to bed, they enjoyed an undisturbed sleep. As they slept so soundlessly, none of them felt the earth tremor or heard the explosive boom in the middle of the night.

Ben was the first to awaken. He felt something as light as a feather tickle his nose and then his cheek. He brushed it away, but within seconds it was back again. He was getting irritated. He swept his face clean again, but just as quickly it was back again. *'Could be flies or ants?'* he thought. He sat up suddenly, shouting, "Get off me!" hands flapping across his face. There were no flies, ants or insects to be seen, but instead feathery, grey ash was dropping out of the sky and weaving its way through the confusion of monkey puzzle branches. Away from the trees, the lava was now coated in a layer of ash and was gunmetal grey, reminding him of a poorly-tuned television. The air was thick with the pungent and putrid smell of burning.

Awoken by Ben's shout, the others were sitting up now, rubbing their bleary eyes. They looked around in amazement at the ash falling like snow. It felt like the middle of the night, as the ash cloud was blocking out the sun. The atmosphere was one of foreboding and menace, and even the chatty parakeets had fallen silent.

"It looks like the end of the world," exclaimed Ben. The others could not blame him for thinking so.

"A volcano must have erupted in the night," said Jack. "I can't believe that we slept through it."

"My memory might be hazy," said Flo, "but from

what I can remember from my geography lessons, the venting of ash comes just before a full-on eruption. We better get out of here."

"That's good enough for me," replied Bella, quickly throwing together her things. "Not that we did geography at school. It wasn't deemed a core subject for young ladies."

Within minutes, after quickly stuffing some 'liquorice' pods in the bags, they were on their way. As soon as they left the protection of the monkey puzzle trees, they realised the abnormality of their situation. They found themselves in the midst of an ash storm, and visibility dropped like a closing curtain to just two metres. Choking, they waded through the swirling, grey sea of ash rising above their knees. It was like walking through treacle. Every three steps, they had to stop to catch their breath, before blindly staggering on. The heat was intense and their clothes were starting to smoulder. Given his size, Ben was finding the journey the toughest as the ash was nearly up to his waist. The ash storm continued to intensify.

"I can't go on," whimpered Ben. Bent double and his body racked by a severe bout of coughing, he appeared like he was standing in sinking sand as the ash steadily climbed up his body.

"Bro, you must keep going," muffled Flo.

"I can't. I simply can't," whined Ben. Determinedly, he took a step forward only to collapse with exhaustion again.

"Ben, I'll carry you," said Jack heroically. "Jump on

my shoulders just like when you were picking the seed pods."

'BANG...' thundered and echoed through the suffocating air. The earth shook and Ben was nearly knocked off Jack's shoulders. The massive explosion parted the ash cloud like a curtain to reveal a spitting cauldron of molten magma high up on the dome of the volcano. Red light fireworks shot into the air, and flaming lava started to spill down the steep slopes.

"We must move quicker and higher," shouted Jack above the roar. Wading and stumbling, they forced their way through, digging their hands deep into the ash to speed up their progress. Through the swirling haze, they spotted a copse of monkey puzzle trees about 200 metres further up the slope. Their pace was tortuously slow and exhaustion was setting in. This time they could not rely on any animals for their survival – they had scarpered long ago. They had only the trees to save them. With one last supreme effort, they made it to the trees, and collapsed coughing and spluttering on to the ground. They turned to see the molten lava spewing and flooding down the slope as fast as a galloping race horse. They watched in horror as their monkey puzzle island was crushed and swallowed up by the flaming lava, and some trees were sent somersaulting down the slope.

Chapter 9 - Andean Watershed

"What a lucky escape. It is going to be another day of expecting the unexpected," said Jack. "Let's keep climbing away from the lava and ash." As they clambered up the steep slope, at times they were forced to be on all fours, grabbing hold of rocks and dirt to help them up. The air started to freshen, so they took in deep breaths to clear their lungs. They had left the monkey puzzle trees behind and were now entering an emerald green forest of dwarf beech trees. Soon, these gave way to a grey wall of treacherous scree leading up to the horizon and what looked like the summit. It was tough going. They had to climb in one horizontal line, as anybody left behind would be bombarded by a cascading waterfall of small, jagged rocks. At times, they would take a step and then slide two steps back. On all fours, they dug their toes into the scree and then reached with their hands to grab the unstable rocks. Bella, her nails now worn and chipped, her hands bloodied, lost her footing and slid 50 metres back down the slope. She let out a cry of exasperation and stamped her foot in frustration only to slip further down. Ben could not suppress a giggle.

Bella, red in the face and bristling with anger, shouted up, "It is all very well for you to giggle. Just like remember your like tantrum in the ash."

"At least she has lost none of her fighting spirit,"

whispered Flo, as Jack headed downwards to offer his help.

Jack offered his hand, and Bella looked at it as if it might bite her. She fell again and this time she reached for Jack's hand. He dragged her steadily up the scree, and eventually, together, they reached the horizon, which thankfully meant the summit.

"Thank you," whispered Bella to Jack, not intending for the others to hear. Flo overheard and thought to herself that it was indeed a day of expecting the unexpected.

Here, on top of the Andes, they felt like they were on top of the world. They looked back the way that they had just come. Beyond the plumes of ash, the flowing lava and the islands of monkey puzzle trees, lay the thick, green forests of beech and rhubarb and the torrential rivers and mighty, sweeping glaciers. Ahead, down the other side, was nothing but desert, stretching as far as the eye could see. The only distinguishing features were the different shades of brown.

"It's a watershed," declared Flo.

"A water what, sis?" asked Ben, looking at her as if the altitude was playing tricks on her mind.

"A watershed," explained Flo. "I learnt about it in geography, but I never thought that I would actually see one. Clouds drenched in water come steaming in from the west across what must be the Pacific. They hit the Andes and drop their load and, 'voila', one side is green from all the rain, and the other is brown and parched from the lack of rain."

"That makes a lot of sense," said Jack, "but now is decision time. North is along the ridge of the Andes, so we need to decide whether we take our chances on the green or the brown side."

"I vote the desert," said Bella. "It's like flat and I am fed up with crossing glaciers and icy rivers and contending with erupting volcanoes. I am like craving some heat."

"But with heat comes a lack of water and food," pointed out Flo.

"Can't we just stay walking on this ridge?" asked Ben. "Surely that will be quicker and we can have the best of both worlds?"

"Too risky," replied Jack. "We are too exposed, and feel how laboured our breathing is. The air is too thin and the altitude sickness might get us. Speaking of which, we must decide which side now, as it is dangerous to sleep at such a height."

The decision was left to fate with an elaborate game of four way, 'rock, paper, scissors'. Bella emerged the winner, and unsurprisingly chose the desert.

Unbeknown to them at the time, they had lingered too long at the top. During the effort of reaching the summit across the steep scree, Ben had got hot and had stripped down to his T-shirt. He had stayed in this state of undress while waiting for Bella and while on the summit. By the time they got going again, he was shivering with cold.

"Ben, put your hoodie back on," commanded Flo. "You'll catch your death of cold." Untying the hoodie from around his waist, Ben slipped it on over his head.

"I reckon that we have no more than one hour of daylight left," warned Jack. It was now 5.30 and the sun was hanging low in the sky. As they descended, it was not long before they lost the sun altogether, as it disappeared behind the jagged ridge. It was not just a race against the fading light, but accelerated by a chilly wind, the temperature was dropping dramatically. Ben's shivering was getting progressively worse. He was shaking uncontrollably and his face had gone ashen.

To make matters worse, he was starting to talk gibberish (even more so than usual), slurring his words and hallucinating. As he stumbled from side to side down the mountain, he mumbled, "Put me to bed, sis. In my big, dippy and soft bed at home with that carved dragon. My room with stars on the ceiling and planets on the wall. Tuck me with up with Pluto. Oh… my downy pillow." With that, he curled up contentedly on the rocky slope.

"Hypothermia," said Jack alarmed, "we must keep him awake." He gently picked up Ben. His breathing was slow and shallow.

Flo softly tapped his face, "Come on, Ben. Wake up, wake up."

His eyelids fluttered. "Let me sleep… I'm so cosy back in my own bed," he mumbled drowsily.

His head dropped forward as he fell back to sleep. "Ben, Ben, please…" pleaded Flo, again gently tapping his face.

Ben's eyes shot open in alarm, "Where am I? I'm just so cold."

Jack took Ben under his arm, and started to haul him down the mountain. "Leave me alone!" said Ben groggily.

"We must find some shelter and get warm soon," warned Jack.

"Here, Ben can have my jumper," said Bella.

"Thanks Bella," said Flo gratefully.

They were losing light and long, ominous shadows stretched down the mountainside. The slopes were barren and bare, with only the occasional hardy shrub bent double against the prevailing wind. Suddenly, a high-pitched scream broke through the impending gloom. Then a series of more plaintive screams. These were returned by a deeper, more distant, reassuring hum. They moved slowly towards the closer screams and they stumbled across a single baby alpaca. The baby was lost and desperately calling out for her mother.

"Where are you?" she cried.

"I'm here," came a distant comforting hum.

The baby led them to a herd of 21 alpacas.

The alpacas were busy getting ready for the night. Scratching at the hard earth to soften it up, the adults were preparing for a good sleep. The children watched while the doting mother of the lost baby made up her bed. The arrival of the children did not seem to surprise or upset them. Dressed in shaggy fur coats in different shades of white and brown, the alpacas looked at them

with their large, expressive eyes that seemed to exhibit both childlike curiosity and wisdom. They seemed to be saying, *'You're welcome to join us.'*

The baby was lying now, snuggling up to her mother. Jack hauled Ben over and put him down beside the mother and baby. Ben was still muttering incoherently, but within minutes he was nestling into the thick fur coats, and he fell asleep. His breathing had become deeper and he was shaking less.

"We need to make a fire to boil some water," said Jack. "A hot drink will help warm Ben up."

They woke Ben to give him a drink infused with herbs they had found in the rhubarb forest. While Ben slept the sleep of angels, the others feasted on liquorice seed pods and warmed their hands around herb tea.

Flo did not sleep a wink. She felt, as an elder sister, responsible for Ben, and she would not forgive herself if something happened to him. She remembered the last thing her parents said to her as the ship was about to leave Buenos Aires, *"Look after your little brother for us."* Ben had overheard and retorted, *"Less of the little, I am perfectly capable of looking after myself."* Now sitting by Ben, Flo monitored his every breath. It was erratic, to say the least – at times short and sharp, at others long and sonorous. Occasionally, he would toss and turn, before nestling back in the thick, soft coats of the alpaca. Once, he cried out, "I want my Mummy." It was a long and tortuous night for them both.

Flo must have finally drifted off for when she awoke the sun was just starting to peak over the horizon. The ray of sunlight first hit Ben, then started to spread over the sleeping throng of alpacas and children. Nobody stirred, and Ben was still breathing. Flo was alone in her thoughts as she looked down at the endless desert below. Their biggest challenge was going to be water – Flo remembered that you can live without food for weeks, but without water for only a couple of days.

Surely there must be an oasis hiding away in the desert, with water, animals and even humans? She felt a guardian angel was looking out for them and if it had not been for the alpacas, Ben for one would not have made it. She did not think she would have been able to go on without her little brother.

She looked at the others. Jack was lying mouth open, catching flies (not that there were any insects at this altitude!) with his head resting on the rump of an alpaca. They could not have made it this far without Jack helping and encouraging Ben through the ash and down the mountain. He had also saved his life when crossing the torrential river. Flo wished that Jack did not always feel the need to prove himself, maybe he was the victim of pushy parents, and was never quite meeting their expectations. By contrast, Bella lay on her side, curled up in the foetal position. She looked vulnerable and scared. It was fair to say that she had been a nightmare at the start, always whinging, complaining and finding fault. In the last two days, she had started to mellow – she had led them across the river and had given her jumper to Ben last night. From comments Bella made, it was clear to Flo that, so far, she had endured an unhappy childhood – unloved by her parents and finding it hard to make friends at school. They were a maverick gang, and it would be a miracle for them to make it out of Patagonia alive. The alpacas started to stir, and Flo was jolted back to reality.

Ben started to come to, wearily rubbing his eyes. "Where am I?" he murmured groggily. He reached out his hands and ran them through the fur coat of the baby alpaca. "And that is certainly not Pluto," he said, as he raised himself up on his hands, hazily taking in the sprawled bodies of the sleeping alpacas and the mountainside beyond. He looked puzzled and turned to Flo, "I must have dreamt that I was back home."

"You did," confirmed Flo.

"I remember feeling so so cold, and then I was back in my own bed at home."

Chapter 10 - Haunted by Ghosts

Jack and Bella started to stir, and they were relieved to see Ben back on his feet again and making sense. The alpacas, warmed by the sun, were starting to stretch their limbs and clamber to their feet. The children looked into their big, supercilious eyes and thanked them for looking after them. They were so much more friendly than the guanacos - instead of spitting, they purred as the children stroked them. It was not long before they were heading up the mountain and waving goodbye; the children headed downwards towards the desert.

They filled up their water bottles from a small mountain stream and, within 20 minutes, they were on the edge of the arid desert plain. It was early morning and already the temperature was starting to soar. With the compass set on north, they looked at the challenge ahead of them. It was a wilderness. A parched and barren land devoid of life and colour stretched out ahead of them. Only an occasional scrub bush, tuft of grass, or outcrop of rock existed to mark their progress. As they walked, the sun beat down relentlessly, and a heat haze rose from the ground. There was no escaping it in this gently undulating landscape of sand, rocks and spruce.

"I think that we must be the only, like, livings things

around," said Bella helpfully. "I wish now that I'd voted for the other side of the Andes."

"The grass is always greener on the other side," said Jack ironically, happy with his joke. Flo laughed, but Bella carried on oblivious.

"I wish I was like a glass half full person. I always seem to see the worst like in every situation and like every person for that matter. I simply cannot help it," said Bella openly.

'Just like saying 'like' all the time,' Flo grinned to herself.

"We had noticed," replied Jack. "Now the positives are that it is warm and not cold, it is relatively flat, and there are no rivers to cross."

With those reassuring words, they started to trudge across the sand.

It was not long before Jack cried, "Oh no. Damn, damn, damn..." The others stopped in their tracks. "I don't have the emergency pack. I must've left it by the mountain stream."

"What an idiot," said Bella helpfully.

"We must go back," said Jack, stating the obvious and refusing to rise to Bella's jibe. "It's got the claw and skin in it..."

"Not to mention the compass, pan and first aid kit," pointed out Flo.

"And the last chunks of chocolate," added Ben, licking his lips.

Heads bowed, they followed their footsteps in the sand and back towards the foothills. Suddenly, Flo knelt down.

"Look at this," she said, with a tremble in her voice. They all looked closer. There was a series of paw prints covering their footprints.

"We are being stalked," said Flo. They jumped to their feet and fearfully looked around. Nothing... nothing in all directions as far as the eye could see.

"It might be that monster," stammered Ben, "wanting its claw back."

"More likely a puma, bro," said Flo.

"Are they dangerous?" asked Bella.

"If they are hungry," replied Flo. "They are usually more partial to alpacas. It must have followed us down the mountainside."

When they returned to the foothills, they all decided to return to the mountain stream. Strength in numbers in front of the prying eyes of the wild cat. They all had an overwhelming sense of being watched.

When they finally returned to the desert, they had lost much valuable time. The desert was now a furnace. Their throats quickly became parched, so all conversation ceased. To beat the boredom and monotony, they each escaped into a world of daydreams. Jack was scoring a century for England. He was coming in at four wickets down and two hundred and fifty runs needed for victory to win the Test series against Australia. Logic dictated caution, but he set about taking apart the Aussie attack. He relived every shot – a sweeping on-drive, a scything hook and a six straight over the bowler's head. His match-winning innings lasted four hours.

Bella was at her school prom. In her black, satin dress, she really was 'belle of the ball' and had also been voted Prom Queen, making her the most popular girl in her year group. At her side was rugby captain, Charlie, tall and charming. Together, they descended the steps and, surrounded by a cheering crowd, they took the first dance to 'This is me' from 'The Greatest Showman'.

By contrast, Flo was out camping in Scotland with her parents and Ben. They had just kayaked across a loch and they had pitched their tents on a sandy beach. The waters were like glass, but occasionally a trout would rise for the evening fly, sending ripples across the surface. Swallows swooped to sip the water, silhouetted against a flaming red sky. On the fire, they were cooking shellfish – mussels, clams and oysters – that they picked up from the beach.

Ben was being naughty at school. At home, he had been breeding pet mice so he could scare the teachers. He had a particularly strict English teacher who was always rattling on about his handwriting and spelling – *"How do you expect me to mark your work if I can't read it? You must remember it is 'i' before 'e', accept after 'c'."* She was always on his back and got on his nerves. One day, he brought a pet mouse into school, and placed it along with a piece of cheese in Miss Craddock's top drawer beside the board markers. She arrived, hair pinched in a bun and looking like she had just eaten a lemon. "Now class, today we have a spelling test. I hope you have all taken the time to learn them," she said with sneer. She reached for a board pen, "Now, write the date in the left..." suddenly, her hand recoiled from the drawer, and she looked down and let out a high-pitched scream, before climbing up on her chair. Her mouth opened and closed like a fish, but no sound came out of her lips. The silence was blissful and they had no spelling test that day.

It was good timing, for just as Ben's daydream had finished, he tripped over flat on his face. He staggered up and dusted himself down, only to take one step and then fall again. He had hit something hard and his toe hurt. He looked down and saw a straight piece of metal glinting in the sun. Kneeling down, he ran his hand down the metal, parting the sand as he did so. The metal rail ran on and on. He looked back to where he had first tripped and he saw another glint of metal. He looked up and the others had carried on, oblivious. Jack was waving his arms around as if he was practising his cricket shots, Bella was dancing with an imaginary partner, while Flo was staring wistfully into space.

"Stop, look what I have found!" shouted Ben.

The other children seemed to come out of a trance and turned slowly round, before heading back to a kneeling Ben.

"Look, there are some metal rails buried in the sand!" said Ben excitedly. "Where there is metal, there must be humans."

The others fell to their knees and started to dig with their hands. More metal rail, but digging deeper they discovered a series of wooden planks.

"It could just be an abandoned railway line," said Jack. "There is hope for us yet. Let's follow it." He checked the compass. "It's heading northeast."

"It is reassuring that humans have been here before us," said Flo, "but it does look like it has been disused for some time. Why would someone go to so much trouble to build a railway line in the middle of nowhere?"

"It could be a mining company," said Bella. "My father's a banker and he often talked about investing in mining companies in this part of the world. Always located far off the beaten track, and he would always send someone else. Father and mother prefer the glitz and glamour of cities."

Following the railway line was easier said than done. Buried in the sand in this featureless landscape, they would start on the wooden sleepers between the rails, but soon they found they would veer off track. It was slow and tortuous progress having to stop every 20 metres to dig for the rails.

"This is simply not working," said Jack. "Let's look for a clue on the horizon, this track must lead somewhere." Looking northwards, their eyes scanned the vast expanse of featureless desert. They looked and looked, but nothing seemed to be out of the ordinary – the odd spruce bush, an occasional outcrop of rock and lots and lots of sand.

It was Bella who broke the silence, "Look, look over there! That distant rocky outcrop seems to be scarred."

Following Bella's pointing finger, they all saw what she meant. The rocks did appear to be scarred, but not in a naturally eroded way. The scars were straight and chiselled.

"We have nothing to lose," said Jack. "Let's head for it."

The trouble with walking across a desert is that it is very difficult to gauge distance. What may seem about two hours walk away, in reality will be double this. This desert was no different. They had thought the outcrop was 90 minutes way, but after two hours of walking it seemed only slightly closer. Encouragingly, when they did check for the rails, they were close by, buried in the sand.

"My eyes may be deceiving me," said Flo, "but I think I can see some buildings at the foot of the rock." They all strained their eyes and yes, they could just make out the triangular shape of some roofs. Drinking the last of their water and excitedly picking up the pace, they closed in on their destination – their sanctuary, their survival and their ticket back home. It was like a developing photograph in a dark room. First the roofs, then the brown walls and black windows, lining the dusty streets. They started to distinguish the buildings – could that be a church? Is that the school?

"There's the station!" cried Flo excitedly. Sure enough, sitting just outside the village, was a building with a green corrugated iron roof with a raised platform. "And there's the train" she continued. Stopped just outside the station was an engine pulling eight carriages loaded up with piles of white rocks.

Hope and happiness spread through the children. Their survival and ticket out of Patagonia was just touching distance away.

"They are in for the shock of their lives," said Jack. "I'm sure it is not every day that four children appear from the desert."

"I bet we look quite a state," said Bella. "I'm still haunted by my face in the mirror at Cape Horn."

"We probably stink as well," said Ben.

"Speak for yourself," replied Bella.

"I just hope that they are as kind and friendly as the animals and birds," said Flo.

As they approached, they started to fantasise about what they might first do on arrival.

"I don't know about you, but the first thing I'm going to do is have a long cold drink and sit in the shade," said Jack.

"I'm going to have a long, cool bath," said Bella. "I simply cannot wait to get out of these smelly clothes."

"I hope that they have a telephone," said Flo. "I cannot wait to ring home. Our parents must be worried sick."

"Well, while you are on the phone, I'll be tucking into a big, juicy burger and chips, washed down with an ice cold Coke."

As they drew ever closer, they soon realised something was not right. No sound came from the village – no barking dog, no hammer on rock, no overheard conversation and no hum of machines. Only an eerie silence. No people, dogs or cats ambled through the streets. No smells of human habitation – cooking food, burning wood, diesel fumes.

They first arrived at the station. They had expected to see the shining railway tracks stretching northwards off into the horizon. It was soon clear that this rusty train, together with its cargo of white rocks, was going nowhere. The rails ahead were also buried in sand. They could just make out the words 'Tamel Aike' on the faded, peeling wooden sign and the green corrugated iron roof of the station flapped tremulously in the gentle breeze. The platform was fractured and cracked, and they watched as family of desert mice emerged blinking from a hole and scurried off in search of food. The place reeked of dereliction and neglect.

Disconsolately, they headed towards the village. They clung on to the hope that even though the station was abandoned, people could still be living there. The houses were all a terracotta brown with walls made of mud and clay tiles making up the roofs. They spotted movement at the end of the main street. Plumes of dust rose in the air, and through this cloud they could just make out the silhouettes of nine figures about 1.5 metres tall. They were struck by their long necks and large protruding bottoms. As the dust settled, a flock of mottled grey rheas (Patagonian's answer to the ostrich) emerged at the bottom of the street and strutted sedately towards them with their chests puffed out. On seeing the children, they took fright. Squawking, they turned and fled in a rolling run resembling the movement of a professional American

footballer. This was not the welcome the children had been expecting.

They followed the rhea tracks into a roofless house. This was clearly where the rheas set up home. The smell of poo was overwhelming, but they did find a nest with four greenish-yellow large eggs about the size of a pineapple.

"Supper this evening," said Flo, collecting them up.

"I hope they like taste better than the penguin eggs," retorted Bella.

"Bound to, there're no fish around here," replied Flo.

Hopes, dreams and fantasies shattered, they continued to explore. They walked into what must have been the school. Dusty exercise books were still open on the notched wooden desks, their pages gently fluttering as the door creaked open. Ink pens, long dried up, lay discarded on the books. Flo looked more closely, and noticed that sentences and pictures were half finished. There was writing on the chalkboard. Faded but just legible was the date, 19 May 1940, and fainter still was what looked like the remnants of a spelling test. More prominent were four names scratched with vigour into the blackboard: Dylano, Aurea, Maria and Inigo. The cushion on the teacher's chair had now become a nest for mice. Chairs littered the classroom; some broken and splintered, others lying prone on the earthen floor and others tucked neatly behind the desks. Amongst the peeling posters lining the walls was a faded black and white photo of the class. 21 smiling pupils sitting in front of the camera, faces full of hope, potential and expectation.

"It is like a scene from 'The Listeners'," said Flo, breaking the eerie silence.

The others stared at her blankly.

"You know, the poem by Walter de la Mare," continued Flo.

Her audience remained bemused.
Undeterred, Flo started to recite;

"The traveller stood perplexed and still.
But only a host of phantom listeners
That dwelt in the lone house then
Stood listening in the quiet of the moonlight
To that voice from the world of men..."

"Well, I don't know much about poetry," interrupted Jack. "What I do know is that they left in a real hurry. What possibly could have caused them to leave so suddenly?"

"Do you think it was some sort of like plague or disease?" suggested Bella, covering her mouth with her hand.

"Maybe it has something to do with the white rocks," said Flo. "Why go to all that trouble to load the carriages if the train is never going to leave the station?"

"I'm really not bothered," said Ben. "I'm not great fan of classrooms, but this one takes some beating. I don't like it, it's really spooky." With that, he turned and quickly walked out the door. The others followed.

The remains of the church was located next door. A cross, leaning awkwardly sideways, sat precariously above the porch. On entering, they saw that the large arch windows had shattered, smothering the six rows of pews in glass. The altar lay covered in a tattered, white cloth, held down by a rusty cross and candles burnt to the wick. The empty pulpit was reflected in the murky waters of the stone font.

"Judging from the number of pews," said Jack. "This must have been a village of 50 or so people."

Bella brought their thoughts back to the future. "Well, so much for all our like fantasies. What are we going to do now?" she asked.

"Our first priority is water," replied Jack. "I think I noticed a well beside the house with the rheas." A circular brick wall topped by a corrugated iron roof encased the well. A rusty bucket hung dangling on a hook and they lowered it into the depths. They were reassured to hear a splash and up came a bucketful of brownish, tepid water. It looked far from inviting.

"What if it was this, like, very same water that, like, killed off this village?" said Bella, ever the pessimist.

"Well, we'll just have to take our chances," said Jack. "We have no more water and we still have a desert to cross. But first we stay here for the night."

"No way, this place is spooky," Ben pleaded.

"We need shelter. It gets so cold in the desert at night," Jack explained.

"I don't believe you."

"Jack's right," interjected Flo. "The heat simply disappears at night and we don't have the clothes or the equipment to survive."

They chose to sleep in the school. At least they could relate to the classroom and it seemed the less alien of all the other properties in the village. They feasted on large rhea eggs – they had the same taste and texture as chicken eggs – accompanied by tuna. They had found an old rusty tin in the village shop that had fallen down behind the shelves.

"All very Cordon *Blue*," said Bella.

"Yes, a banquet fit for Kings and Queens," agreed Jack, as they sat around the teacher's table.

"I don't care what you say," said Ben. "Nothing will ever beat a burger and chips."

They resisted the temptation of Quaker Porridge Oats. A tatty, mice-nibbled box had also been discovered in the shop. They decided to leave this treat until the next morning.

In the shelter of the classroom, all the children slept soundly apart from Flo. She endured a fitful night's sleep filled with vivid dreams.

She dreamt that she was Aurea – one of the names etched on the board.

'The morning had started as any other. My father went off early to the mine to beat the searing temperatures, while my mother cooked breakfast of scrambled rhea eggs. Dressed in immaculate white school uniform, my brother and I waved goodbye to mother and headed off on the short walk to school. It was noisy outside, the air was alive with the mechanical drills in the mine, and I imagined my father stripped to the waist even at this early hour, chipping away at the hard, unforgiving rock. Plumes of dust spiralled in the air. Over at the station, a truck, with a clash of brakes and pistons, was unloading saltpetre from the mine onto the train.

Tuesday was a good day at school. Geography, History and then Spanish, and the bonus being no Maths and Science.

I liked playing with language and travelling the world, but I simply could not get to grips with numbers. They were alien to me. I was confident about the spelling test today, as I had taken the time to learn them.

So, with a skip in my step, I headed through the school door. My brother was hesitant and reluctant, and I knew that he would prefer to be playing outside in this sunny weather rather than being enclosed in the mud walls. I liked my teacher, Miss Lopez. She was so kind and patient (even with my brother!) and seemed to know everything across all subjects from Maths to Spanish. I wished that I had her knowledge.

The morning passed without incident, until they were starting the spelling test, when the hum of the mine machinery suddenly stopped. 'Surely it could not be lunchtime already' she thought. The clock on the classroom wall read 11.52.

"Now the first word is 'llama'," said Miss Lopez. (Flo's Spanish was not good enough to dream in full sentences, only single words!).

"Is that the animal or the name?" asked one bright spark.

"Very clever, choose either, they are both spelt the same," replied Miss Lopez, with the patience of a saint. 'The next word is 'escuela'."

The humming of the machinery had been replaced by a crescendo of voices – shouts, cries, angry outbursts. By the time they had got to their seventh spelling, the whole village seemed to be in uproar. Miss Lopez stopped the spelling test and ushered the children out to see what all the commotion was about.

It was almost as if the miners were being spewed out of the earth. As they exited out of the gates, they looked dejected and sad, however, there was also a tinge of anger in their eyes. I rushed up to my father and he wrapped his muscular arms around me.

"The mine is closing," he said with resignation. "They don't need us or the saltpetre we mine anymore. We have lost the reason to live here."

"But it's my home," I said, "I was born here. What about my friend, my brother..."

"With no mine, there is no money," he replied. "The village is closing and we all have to leave."

"But when – a week, a month?" I asked anxiously.

"The last train goes tomorrow," he said, with finality.

There was thus no time for the children to go back for their school books as they rushed back home to pack their worldly belongings. This ghost village was freeze framed, caught in a snapshot of time, the moment the words were uttered, 'THE MINE IS CLOSING'. Open books on school desks, teacher's writing on the chalkboard, sacred water in the font, hymn books on the church pews, dirty plates in the sink, a can of tuna dropping behind a shelf...'

Once they were all awake, Flo recounted her dream. This seemed like a plausible explanation, even though none of the children had heard of saltpetre before.

Looking out the classroom window, Jack said, "There is certainly nothing else to keep you here other than a mine. It really is the middle of nowhere." His words highlighted again the enormity of the task that again lay ahead of them. More desert to cross without an abandoned train line to guide them.

Chapter 11 Mystical Desert

"I think that this village is like trying to tell us something," said Bella. "This desert is no place for us. I know I like voted for it, but I think we should take our chances on the other side."

"Great minds think alike," agreed Jack. "I was thinking exactly the same thing. Anywhere has got to be better than this unforgiving desert." This time round the children were all in agreement.

The Andes (and water) did not look far away, no more than a day's walk. Fuelled by porridge and rhea eggs, and carrying as much brownish water as possible, they decided to head off on a bearing of northwest. In theory, this would mean that they might bypass some rivers on the other side. While they had viewed the desert from the village, it had all looked flat, but it was not long before their way was barred by sand dunes. Climbing them was thirsty and energy-sapping work. The sand was up to their knees, and it was like wading through granulated honey. They were forced to run up the dunes to avoid sinking too deeply into the sand. Ben, in particular, enjoyed sliding down the other side, but the respite was short lived, as they were confronted by wave upon wave of dunes. Up, down, up, down... and the temperature was starting to rise. Through the heat haze, they could just make out the blurred image of the Andes. They looked no closer.

They waded, climbed up yet another dune. The view from the top took their breath away. Below them, stretching as far as the eye could see, was a desert plain full of craters dusted with white silt, littered with dramatic sandstone rock formations.

"It looks the Valley of the Moon mixed with Alice in Wonderland," said Flo dreamily.

None of the children had been to the moon, but they had read Alice in Wonderland, and they knew exactly what she meant. The coarse, white, rugged surface looked exactly how the surface of the moon might look, and the towering rock structures were in the shape of mythological objects and living things. In the far distance, they could see a fairy castle perched on the top of a sheer rock face; to their right, a sphinx was sitting back on its haunches; off to their left, a monk was kneeling in prayer and just below, the three Magi floated across the craters on camels. It was a truly strange and magical scene.

It was Ben who bought them back down to earth. "Look over there," said Ben, pointing. "There's a massive Coke bottle. And look, there's one of my favourite cartoon characters, Deputy Dawg."

"Like who the hell is that?" asked Bella.

"Are you kidding me?" replied Ben. "He's the dog cowboy sheriff that talks in a really funny voice."

They slid down the dune onto the surface of the 'moon'. They crunched across the crusty floor, weaving

their way through the dramatic rock formations. These cast a welcome shade and offered them respite from the strong, scorching north wind. It was dead against them, parching their skin and sucking any moisture from their throats. Their thirst was raging, and a sip of water evaporated on their tongues, offering no relief.

"It's like having a hairdryer permanently in your face, switched to maximum heat and speed," said Bella. "My water is now the temperature of a cup of tea. It is, like, really unpleasant."

Suddenly, they heard the distant sound of thunder. Puzzled, they looked skywards. How could there be thunder on a cloudless day? Then they saw, emerging from behind the fairy castle, a huge, swirling tsunami of sand sweeping towards them.

"Sandstorm!" shouted Jack. "Quick, drop to the ground."

They were just in time as, within seconds, they were being bombarded with sand, stinging their faces, hands and ankles. Lying face down with their hands over their heads, they were plunged into darkness as the storm raged around them. They tried to nestle into the hard ground to protect themselves.

Eventually, the sand did clear, but the powerful wind remained. Jack poked his head up, and, barely audible above the roaring wind, shouted, "We cannot stay here forever. Let's make a run for the sphinx!" The others nodded. Kneeling, and then rising slowly to their feet, they had to bend forwards at 45 degrees just to remain standing up. A gust hit Ben, sweeping him off his feet and sending him sprawling to the ground.

"This is no good!" shouted Jack. "We need to streamline. Line up behind me and hold on to the person in front of you."

With Jack in the lead and Ben sandwiched in the middle, they lined up like a conga. The sphinx was a tantalising 100 metres away. Step by step, they edged their way closer. Soon, an exhausted Jack had to swap places with Bella, and it was not long before Flo took over. They danced the conga all the way to the sphinx and collapsed at her feet.

They sheltered for three hours behind the sphinx. Three precious hours, three hours lost in their quest to reach the Andes and escape the desert. Most worrying was that they were all now low on water. While the storm had descended suddenly, the wind was taking its time to die down. As they emerged, blinking, from the shadow of the sphinx, they witnessed a series of sand whirlwinds sweeping across the desert from their right to left. Beyond them, the Andes looked distant, and there was no way that they were going to reach them by nightfall. Another night in the desert lay ahead of them. They had some rhea eggs and porridge, but with so little water, they could not possibly cook them.

"Let's head for the fairy castle, dodging the dust devils as we go," said Jack. "We'll camp there for the night."

"From a sphinx to a fairy castle through a portal of dust devils – we really are in a dream," replied Flo.

"Some dream," said Bella. "More like a nightmare."

They waited while a dust devil swept across their path, and they then headed out across the desert towards the fairy castle. Their faces, hands and ankles were still smarting from the sandstorm; however, it was such a relief that the wind now was intermittent, its ferocity now contained within the mini tornados. They could also walk upright and stretch out their legs, rather than stumbling along bent double, but occasionally they had to sprint to avoid the sweeping plumes of sand. Walk, wait, sprint... wait, sprint, walk... sprint, walk, wait... they edged their way towards the castle.

"It feels like interval training at school," panted Bella. "I hated it then, and on this sand, it is even worse." She rested, bent downwards, hands resting on her knees, gasping for air.

"Watch out!" cried Ben.

Instinct forced Bella to break into a sprint again. Ben laughed.

They heard an uplift of wind. Just 10 metres above, two falcons were gliding, circling and soaring on the dying thermals of the day. Their dark brown feathers rippled in the wind, and their yellow-orange legs and bills, together with their white throats and necks, gave them a splash of colour. They were close enough to see that their beady black eyes were staring intently at the desert floor. What could they possibly be looking for in such a dry and arid place? As their shadows swept across the sand, the children first heard a scurrying and then they spied two pygmy armadillos scratching around in the ground. They were tiny, about the size of Jack's hand, and they were like no armadillo that the children had ever seen in a zoo or book. Rosy pink shells sat perched on their grey, furry bodies. They looked like moles wearing fancy, armoured headdresses and tasselled capes. Occasionally, they would stop, raise their heads, ears pricked and nose twitching, before returning to their scuffling around. Had they sensed the hunting falcons above? They certainly had not seen them through those minuscule eyes.

The falcons continued to circle. Then suddenly, in a two-prong attack, they dropped like thunderbolts, with talons bared. Just metres away from the unsuspecting armadillos, they spread their wings to break their fall and, reaching out, their claws hooked into the furry body below the pink armour. The armadillos let out a collective squeal as they rose dangling in the air. The

falcons flew skywards over the heads of the children, dropping their prey as they did so. Like manna from heaven, the two pink armadillos landed at the children's feet.

The children looked in amazement. "That was no mistake," said Flo. "They are gifts – our supper for tonight. This place will never cease to surprise."

"You're not seriously saying that we eat these pink, furry things," said Bella, in disgust.

"Suit yourself, it's no different from the other stuff we have eaten," replied Flo. "I remember in the end you actually enjoyed the mushroom."

"These are different, they are living creatures."

"Not anymore," interjected Jack.

By the time the sun started to set, they were close to the fairy castle. The sun was a flaming ball of orange, sending streaks of red and yellow across the sky and turning the desert sand the colour of crimson. Ahead, the silver moon rose suddenly above the castle, bathing the sky and land in a blue light. The children spun around in surprise to discover that their shadow in front had now been joined by an identical shadow behind.

"Wait until I tell my friends," said Ben. "They'll never believe me. Two shadows, pink armadillos, generous falcons, fairy castles and, of course, Deputy Dawg, all in one place."

Above and below, the sun and moon fought a battle of domination: skies of silver blue and flaming red clashed. Even though the children knew the victor, it did not stop them gazing in awe and amazement. The sun was heroic in defeat, for as it sank below the horizon, it let out a green flash and launched a burning comet of red briefly lighting up the sky. Only then did the red tide retreat before the advancing silver blue.

"So that's the legendary green flash," said Jack. "I have never seen it before. Legend has it that all who witness it will have good luck and fortune. Perhaps, just perhaps, we will survive and see our families again."

Having witnessed nature's light show, they set up camp in the shadow of the fairy castle. They foraged scrub bushes, sheltering below the walls, and lit a fire. They first burnt off the grey fur and then let the armadillos cook in their own shells. They tasted of roasted pork, and even Bella could not resist. As they savoured each mouthful, for there was little to go round, they realised that they were not alone. First, it was the sound that alerted them: a series of calls, 'tuco-tuco', 'tuco-tuco', 'tuco-tuco', echoed around them. They then noticed, in the moonlight, gopher-like heads with prominent buck teeth and pricked ears, bobbing up from underground. They would look at them quizzically, before darting back into their burrows.

Their raging thirsts at first dominated their sleep and they dreamt of rivers, lakes, running taps, fizzy water and lemonade. But as the desert temperatures plunged, they were soon dreaming of hot water bottles, electric blankets, down duvets, feather pillows and endless cups of piping hot chocolate. They tossed and turned all night in a desperate attempt to keep warm. They were greatly relieved when the sun finally rose above the sphinx and they could all thaw out their frozen limbs. The 'tuco-tuco' gophers continued to watch them with puzzled looks, as since the mine had closed, they had probably never seen any humans before.

"The Andes do not look much closer than they did yesterday morning," sighed Bella. She was right, they still stood distant across the expanse of sand and rock sculptures.

"If we head off now, I reckon we'll hit the foothills by late afternoon," said Jack optimistically. "By the way, does anybody know what day it is? I have totally lost track."

Silence reigned and it was clear, wrapped up as they were in their quest to survive, none of the children had given this a minute's thought. They had purely existed on a basis of taking each day as it comes.

"Well, when the ship went down it was the night of 14th December," said Flo. "I remember it was nearly 10 days to go until Christmas and our parents were going to join us in Punta Arenas in time to celebrate. I'm not sure what day that was, though."

The children got out their fingers and started to count out loud. First morning with the elephant seals, the next in the cave with the guanacos, followed by the night with burrowing owls beside the glacier. The rhubarb forest was next, then the monkey puzzle island, followed by snuggling up to the alpacas. Then, the shattered hopes of the ghost mining village and finally, here they were below the ramparts of a fairy castle. A journey totalling 8 days. It seemed so much longer, and an adventure that read like 'Alice in Wonderland'.

"So it is the 23rd and Christmas Eve is tomorrow!" exclaimed Jack.

"Well, we certainly cannot be spending Christmas in this like godforsaken desert," said Bella grumpily. "We better get going."

Chapter 12 - Dinosaurs & Grasshoppers

Leaving the fairy castle behind, they again trudged off into the sand. The rock formations did not cease to surprise and amaze them. They passed a submarine seemingly hovering above the shimmering sand, then an eagle perched and primed for a kill, and far off to their left was a dragon breathing fire. It was then that Ben fell flat on his face again.

"What was that?" he exclaimed, rising slowly to his feet and dusting off his knees. He clawed away at the ground to discover it was not a railway track this time. Emerging out of the sand was the rounded joints of a leg bone. Bleached white with age, this could not be the remains of a camelid; it was far too massive.

"Stop!" cried Ben excitedly, "take a look at this." The other children surrounded Ben, and they were soon on their knees digging. They dug and they dug, and the bone seemed to go on for ages before they finally reached the ankle. It took the strength of all four of them to lift the bone out of the sand.

"Was that really worth it?" asked Bella panting. "It is not as if we can eat it or take it home."

"For me, it's an early Christmas present," said Jack. "It has to be a dinosaur. Wait until I tell my father about this."

"Oh, very Indiana Jones,' said Bella sarcastically.

"They're my favourite films."

Surrounded as they were by the strange and magical rock sculptures, the children soon realised that they must be walking on the very ground that the dinosaurs trod all those thousands of years ago. Centuries of erosion by the wind, biting and eating away at the surface, had now revealed the Jurassic layer.

"No wonder Sir Arthur Conan Doyle got his idea for 'The Lost World' from his adventures in Patagonia," said Flo.

"No one will ever believe us," Jack agreed. "The Valley of the Moon one minute, Alice in Wonderland the next followed up by Jurassic Park! All in just two days."

"At least we have each other to confirm the truth," said Bella. It seemed that the strange, magical qualities of Patagonia were starting to take a hold on even the harshest of critics.

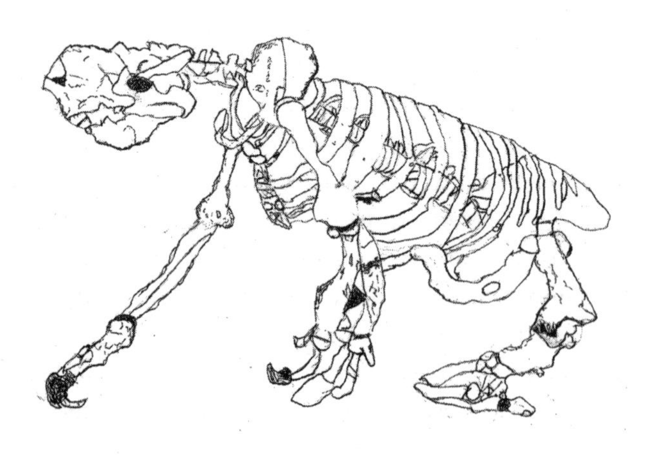

"Let's get on, to find someone to tell," said Jack encouragingly.

Reluctantly, they left the huge dinosaur that would have been a prized exhibit for any museum around the world. The weirdness of the place did not stop there. They passed 50 round stone bowling balls lying in a shallow dip. The balls were perfectly circular and it was as if a game of boules was in progress. They even spotted the jack, significantly smaller than the rest. Stranger still, all around other balls were emerging from the sand, patiently waiting for the wind to release them.

Resisting the temptation to play boules, they soldiered on into the rising temperature of the day. Their water situation was dire, mere sips lying at the bottom of their water bottles. They heard them first, a distant, rhythmic hum. They turned in the direction of the noise and saw a dense, brown cloud sweeping towards them. It was unlike any cloud they had ever seen as it was gliding just centimetres above the ground and rising to two metres. The hum quickly became a roar, and before they could take any evasive action, they were enveloped in a storm of grasshoppers. They were everywhere: entangled in their hair, kicking in their ears, crunching under their feet, pinging off their clothes and trying to land on their eyelashes. The sun was eclipsed by their jumping, writhing bodies, and the children had to fight and carve their way through this shifting sea of long-legged, bulbous-eyed insects. They left as suddenly as they had arrived, and the children watched with

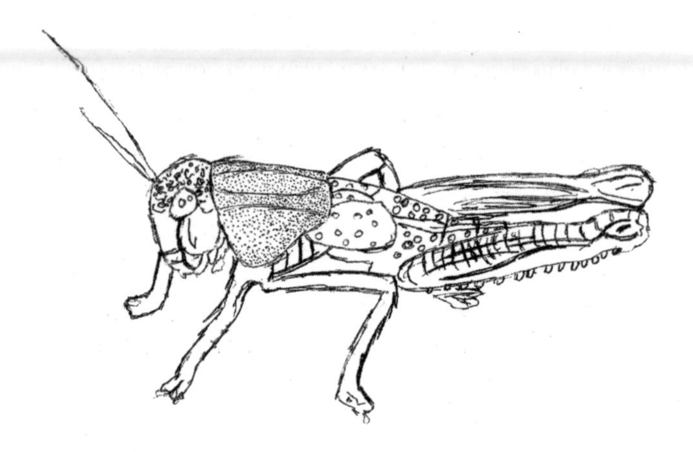

relief as the brown, twitching cloud swept its way towards the hunting eagle.

The only evidence left of the storm was lying at their feet – crippled bodies trampled while they tried to escape the grasshoppers.

Ben picked up one of the deceased for close inspection. 'I wonder if you can eat them?' he asked.

"One of my heroes, Bear Grylls, is always eating insects," replied Jack. "Apparently, they are crunchy and nutritious."

"Indiana Jones one minute and Bear Grylls the next," said Bella. "Can't you, like, live in the real world? Here we are - children stuck a desert, very thirsty and with no food."

"I'm sure they cannot do us any harm," chipped in Flo.

They collected the corpses for what they hoped would be supper in the foothills of the Andes.

They stumbled on through the relentless heat. The rock formations and bowling balls had given way to a featureless expanse of shimmering sand. No shade now from the heat of the sun, and they had all drunk the last of their water. The Andes lay tantalisingly close, but seemed to be getting no closer. Suddenly, Jack broke the silence.

"Look, look over there," said Jack hoarsely, struggling to get the words out between his parched lips.

Stopping, they all turned to see where he was pointing. There, less than a 100 metres away, was a pool of water. They closed their eyes and opened them again to make sure they weren't imagining it. The pool was still there. Excitedly, they reached for their water bottles and ran towards it. The pool hurried away from them, moving when they moved, stopping when they stopped.

"I'm going to get it!" screamed Ben, sprinting headlong at the pool and then clawing frantically at the sand.

"I wouldn't like waste your energy," said Bella. "It's like a mirage."

"What on earth is a mirage?"

Bella huffed and rolled her eyes, while Flo patiently explained the water effect was caused by the shimmering waves of heat rising off the dry ground.

Drunk with fatigue, they staggered on, silent and lost in their individual thoughts, thinking of what they would usually be doing on the day before Christmas Eve. Flo was looking forward to being reunited with her parents in Puerto Montt and Ben was climbing the ladder to put the angel on top of the tree, before shaking all his presents to see if he could guess what was inside. Jack was out tobogganing, rushing downwards at breakneck speed, wind in his hair and snow flying up into his face. A white Christmas was the norm for Bella as they usually went out to their chalet in the Alps. As an only child, she often found herself alone or at ski school. Her mum did not like to ski at this time of year as she found the weather too cold, and her dad did not have the patience to go at her pace. Her parents always said that she could bring a friend. Who was ever going to leave their family at Christmas to join hers? It was strange, but she had never felt less alone, out here attempting to survive alongside Jack, Flo and Ben.

They were jerked out of their daydreams by a flock of flamingos flying overhead. With their elongated necks stretched forward and their long legs and feet pointing backwards, they flew like arrows.

"Where there's flamingos, there's water," said Jack, breaking into a run to follow them. Suddenly, their pink wings tipped with black feathers swerved to the right and they started to circle gracefully into a descent. The children all started to run now up a slight incline and then, just below them, was a shallow, shimmering lake fringed in white.

"Yippee..." shouted Ben. While they sprinted to the shore, the flamingos seemed to stop in mid-air, long necks now pointing skywards and stick-like legs dangling, and they gracefully dropped into the water, took a few pedalling steps, before bending their necks to drink.

Jack was the first to reach the white shore. He stopped suddenly and bent down to touch the white crystals. He licked his finger and his face recoiled in disgust.

"It's salt," he said, through gritted teeth. "It can't be. How can flamingos drink salt water?"

"Maybe it's all evaporated off in the heat," suggested Flo hopefully.

"Let's give it a go," replied Jack, taking off his shoes and then dipping his toes in. "It's boiling hot."

"Great," said Bella, "I'm like dying for a hot bath, I must stink to high heaven."

"Ouch!" screamed Jack, "it stings," and started to hop around like a demented disco dancer. They looked down at the top of his feet, and a flaming red rash was emerging. "I think the water must be toxic."

"But just look at the flamingos," said Bella, as they continued to sip calmly from the lake.

"They must have Teflon legs," exclaimed Jack. "I won't be drinking this water for all the tea in China. I don't care how thirsty I am."

"All this water and not a drop to drink," said Flo reflectively.

"Just, like, our luck," said Bella as, thirstily, they turned their backs on the lake and the flamingos, and headed off to the foothills of the Andes, now just touching distance away.

Soon, their feet left the sand, and they started to rise.

They reached a plateau of spruce grass, and decided to camp there for the night before the slope became too steep. Exhaustedly, Ben threw himself onto the ground and then, with a yelp of agony, he jumped straight back up again, clutching his buttocks.

"What is that?" he howled.

Flo took a closer look and uncovered, nestling in the thin grass, a prickly cactus.

The others all laughed while Ben hopped around. It was a delicate operation for Flo and embarrassing for Ben. He had to drop his pants; his sister meticulously extracted thorn after tiny thorn from his backside. Bella and Jack chose to avert their eyes and ignore the cries of agony.

They had nothing to eat apart from the grasshoppers they had collected in the aftermath of the storm. They dry fried them and tentatively nibbled at their crisp, crunchy bodies. With their mouths like sandpaper from their raging thirsts, this was not the ideal food to be eating. They craved moist, fleshy food that melted in the mouth – a cheese soufflé to start, followed by succulent chicken, finished off with ice cream. Indeed, anything but grasshoppers, especially on the night before Christmas Eve.

"Bizarrely, they seem to taste of deep-fried sardines," said Bella, with a puzzled look on her face. The others looked at her in amazement. Here was the person who had flatly refused to eat the mushrooms, monkey puzzle pods and berries and then, when driven by hunger, had declared them all to be disgusting. Clearly, she was getting a taste for wild, outdoor food. With their thirsts raging, bellies rumbling and breath smelling of sardines, they finally drifted off to sleep dreaming of Christmas trees, tinsel, baubles and snow.

Chapter 13 - Christmas Eve morning

They awoke with the sun. They were desperate to get an early start to climb up over the Andes and get as far as they could down the other side. Who knows, there could be a small village nestling in the Andean foothills just sitting there waiting for them? The residents could this very minute be calmly waking up and mapping out their day – wrap presents, put the final baubles on the tree, prepare the turkey, stuffing and vegetables, and put the lemonade in the fridge.

These thoughts of Christmas were far from Jack's mind. He could not think beyond his splitting headache. Thump, thump, thump… there was a drummer playing noisily and energetically in his head. Despite the going being good and the slope gentle, he could not shake off the ringing in his ears and the throbbing in his head. Suddenly, Jack felt a searing pain in his neck and stars started to float across his vision. Dizzily, he stumbled and it took all his strength and balance to stay upright. Trailing behind the others, he opened his mouth to cry out. No sound escaped his lips and he collapsed to his knees. He then fell forward, face down and unconscious in the dirt.

"Jack!" shouted Bella, sprinting down frantically to his prone body. Flo and Ben joined her, to find Jack muttering incoherently and his eyes rolling in their sockets.

"Jack, Jack, come back to us," urged Bella, gently tapping his face.

Jack blinked and his eyes stopped. "Where am I?" he muttered, barely audible.

"What's wrong with Jack?" asked Ben, looking horrified. Here was their leader and his saviour on several occasions, seemingly out for the count.

"It could be altitude sickness," said Flo. "It can hit even the strongest and fittest."

"Is there a cure?" pleaded Ben.

"I think the best thing to do is go down," replied Flo hesitantly.

They all, with the exception of Jack, looked back down the mountain. The desert beckoned to them like the jaws of death, the mouth of hell. It was not an option on a normal day, least of all Christmas Eve...

"We will have to carry him," urged Bella. He was too heavy for a piggyback. Bella and Flo bent down, crossed and linked arms, while Ben tried to slide Jack on to this makeshift seat. Barely conscious, Jack was no help whatsoever. Eventually, Ben pulled him into position, the girls just about managed to stumble to their feet. Ben held Jack's limp body up. They staggered ten paces, before realising that this was hopeless. They all slumped to the ground, holding their heads in their hands in despair and exhaustion. They had come so far... they could not give up now.

Bella was the first to look up. She realised they were not alone. Animal tracks criss-crossed the foothills and not far away was a steaming mound of poo.

Bella walked over to investigate. There was no escaping it, this pile of brown, spherical shaped droppings looked just like something Hero would produce. Hero, her stallion back home, her confidante, her escape, her best friend.

"Horses," pronounced Bella. "There are horses nearby."

"They are bound to be wild," said Flo.

"They are our only chance and, trust me, I have a way with horses," replied Bella.

They heard some neighing and, leaving Jack sitting in the dirt, they climbed over a crest in the hill to find a herd of seven horses pulling at the sparse, withered grass. They were wild and skittish and, unlike the other animals, they looked nervous at the sight of the children. Bella chose a dark chestnut with a slightly curving white nose and matching white socked feet, which made him look as if he were dancing when he moved.

But it was his mahogany eyes that attracted Bella most – they were intelligent, kind and placid.

Making chuckling, cooing noises, Bella slowly approached the chestnut. Their eyes were locked on each other. Suddenly, with a twist of his neck, he trotted off, following the others who had already taken fright. Undeterred, Bella followed and he kept stopping to meet her gaze. Bella edged ever closer – 10 metres, 5 metres, 3 metres, 1 metre – and then their game of cat and mouse ended with her running her fingers through his mane.

Bella led the chestnut down to Jack and together they hauled him up onto the horse's back. The chestnut seemed to sense their objective, and it was he who led the way upwards along a twisting animal track. They made good progress. The air was becoming cooler and fresher, but at the same time, it was noticeably thinner. Their breathing was becoming more laboured and, at more frequent intervals, they had to stop to catch their breath. The soft ground and the track gave way to tumbling, cascading granite scree. This scree was beyond the strength and agility of the chestnut, and reluctantly they parted company, but they had gained precious height. At the same time, some colour was returning Jack's cheeks and his breathing was less ragged. He could now move, but ever so slowly, on his own.

It was steep now, and they were forced on to their hands. They had to move in a line, climbing only at the pace that Jack could muster, as anyone left behind risked being bombarded with jagged pieces of granite. The sardine grasshoppers had not provided much energy and their reserves were at an all-time low. Their legs screamed and their thirst raged. It was tortuous for them all.

They reached what they thought or hoped was the top. Another false summit, their hopes dashed yet again. Just below them lay a glistening, emerald lake edged by steep scree slopes. The far end was shrouded in mist.

Chapter 14 - Crack in the Monoliths

Now it was Ben's turn. "I'm not sure I can go much further," he murmured.

"Come on," encouraged Bella, taking over Jack's role. "It's not much further now."

As if in answer, the clouds suddenly unfurled and parted to reveal three towering granite monoliths reaching up into the sky. The sun hit these sheer and impenetrable walls, turning them a splendid pink. They glowed and seemed to melt the swirling and encroaching cloud around them. Mouths open, silence reigned.

How could a view so beautiful spell such impending doom? Their dreams of Christmas Eve and a welcoming village on the other side evaporated.

Ben echoed all their thoughts, "How on earth are we going to get over those?"

"Good question," said Flo with a sigh.

"Well, we can't go over them, that's for sure," said Bella, "and we don't have the time to go round them."

"We can't go over them," interrupted Ben, "we can't go round them, we can't go under them. The only way is through them. It was in a book Mummy used to read to me."

"Bro, you could just be right," agreed Flo. "Anyway, we are past the point of no return. We could not survive another night without water."

Scanning the three massive towers, they seemed fused together.

Hoping beyond hope, they slowly edged their way around the emerald lake. Jack's head was bowed, and the pain had now spread to his neck. With Jack out of action and barely capable of looking after himself, it was Bella who turned to Ben.

"Give me your hand," she said gently. "It's Christmas Eve, and we need to keep moving." Tentatively, Ben reached out his hand. Bella took it and started to coax Ben across the scree. Flo and Jack, breathing heavily, followed close behind.

They had now reached the far side of the lake. As Bella led Ben up the steep slope towards the granite towers, she suddenly sensed a slight movement out of the corner of her eye. She turned quickly but there was nothing, just an empty expanse of rock and scree. She must have imagined it. Then that movement again off to her right. Nothing. *'Was she imagining it? Was it like the mirage in the desert?'*

Then a fleeting movement, high-pitched whistle and the sound of hoof on rock, and finally Bella spied, camouflaged amongst the rocks, a herd of five cinnamon vicunas. Related to, but much smaller than llamas, alpacas and guanacos, the vicunas are amongst the most timid and elusive animals in Patagonia. Their fur is legendary in quality and silkiness, and once made the robes for Inca kings. This, of course, was of no interest to the children at this present moment in time.

The children watched these miniature camelids, swift and graceful as they jumped from rock to rock before seeming to glide up the scree.

"Let's like follow them," said Bella. "We have not gone far wrong with the animals so far." This was indeed a turn up for the books as invariably Bella had poured cold water on trusting the animals. Could she be mellowing at last? If so, about time too.

"We've got nothing to lose," agreed Flo, leading the way up the scree in the wake of the vicunas. Ben, forgetting his exhaustion, followed close behind, and Jack seemed to have gained some colour back in his cheeks and his headache was less intense. The appearance of the vicunas had brought them the most important feeling of them all – hope.

It was a struggle to keep up. The vicunas glided

gracefully up the steep slope, while the children stumbled and staggered. Looking up after a further 30 minutes of strenuous climbing, it felt as though they were on a wild goose chase as the vicunas neared a solid, sheer granite wall. They stopped to catch their breath, and as they watched, the lead vicuna seemed to disappear, ghost-like, into the granite. Then the second was mysteriously swallowed up, followed by the third and fourth. Only the fifth remained, straggling behind the others.

"Quick, we cannot like lose them," urged Bella, and on all fours, scrambled up the scree. They marked the spot as the lone vicuna followed the others in this magical disappearing act.

"Just when we thought we had seen it all," said Flo. "We now have vanishing vicunas. Vanishing vicunas, it has a nice ring to it."

"Let's like cut the literary alliteration," said Bella. "We need to discover their secret." There was no anger and frustration in tone, just curiosity and an instinct for survival.

They reached the impenetrable granite walls and, steadily, they edged their way around on a narrow ledge.

"We just need to head for where the first and second tower meet," said Bella. Since Jack had been inflicted with altitude sickness, she had assumed the role of leader. They looked up. A solid, granite wall stretched for 30 metres, before separating into giant monoliths soaring up into the sky and piercing the clouds. They

reached the point and noticed a crack running all the way down, which had previously been invisible. Edging around the ledge, they discovered a narrow gap no more than a metre wide leading steeply upwards. So this was the secret behind the vicunas' disappearing trick. There were no words, but they were all thinking the same thing – they never would have found this secret passage without the help of the vicunas.

Like a scene out of Narnia, they turned their backs on the brown desert and disappeared into the granite wall. At times, they had to go sideways as they squeezed their way down the narrow passage, and it became darker and darker with just a sliver of light from above. From ahead and behind them, the darkness enveloped them. The granite was cold and unforgiving and the silence eerie, and a sudden chill of doubt descended upon them. Had they been right to trust the skittish vicunas? Dizzy with the altitude and driven by the thought of Christmas Eve, were the vicunas figments of their imagination? How had they come so far, only to perish in a granite tomb, with no chance of their bodies ever being found?

Despairingly, they groped their way up the tunnel. They squeezed around a bump in the rock, and suddenly they spied a mere slit of light ahead. This grew and grew as they edged their way sideways and then, blinking, they emerged out into the sunshine. They were hit by the colour. After days in the brown shades of the desert and the menacing darkness of the passage, they could not get over the vividness of the emerald green of trees, bushes and plunging grassy valleys streaked with blue. Just 100 metres below them, a crystal blue lake lay huddled in the mountain folds. On the shore, they could just make out a flock of flamingos basking in the late afternoon sun and beside them, with heads bowed lapping at the waters, were the vicunas, their saviours. Above them, two condors glided across the azure on the dying thermals of the day. They now knew how Peter, Edmund, Susan and Lucy must have felt as they stepped out of the gloomy closeness of the wardrobe and into the snowy white of Narnia.

"This is some Christmas present," said Flo in awe.

The breath-taking view revived Jack. The colour returned to his cheeks and his throbbing headache disappeared. He was now ready to assume his role as leader.

"Let's go and get some water," said Jack. "Clearly, we have left the toxic stuff behind us."

Quickly, they scrambled down the mountainside and, within 30 minutes, they were quenching their raging desert thirsts.

"There is no way people could choose not to live in this paradise," said Flo, as she gulped down the cool, refreshing water.

"Heaven," said Bella as, forever ladylike, she sipped away at her water bottle, desperately resisting the temptation to down it in one.

The shadows of the stunted trees surrounding the lake were starting to stretch and lengthen as the sun hung low in the sky. "We'd better keep moving," pointed out Jack, "before we lose the light." Refreshed, they followed a twisting animal track through a forest of miniature beech trees. Their path ran alongside a cascading, babbling mountain stream, and above the sound of the water, they were serenaded by the sweet music of birdsong. A hummingbird hovered feeding on the sweet nectar of an orchid, a flash of blue darted over a deep, limpid pool, and butterflies fluttered and flitted across the sunbeams shooting through the trees. The air was starting to become thick with humidity, which they found comforting after the dryness of the desert. Was all this Nature's gift-wrapped Christmas present to them all? Suddenly, the thought of Christmas did not seem so daunting and threatening. They had Nature and each other, and they would survive to see it in with food and water. Hardly a lavish feast and celebration, but even in their wildest dreams, which had plagued them in the desert, they had not imagined such a heavenly place.

Chapter 15 - Christmas Night

Still at a high altitude, they quickened their pace to beat the setting sun. Ahead, the sky above the plunging valley had turned a crimson red, and the sun blinked on the horizon, then vanished. They scrambled on in twilight and a star appeared low in the sky. It seemed to be beckoning them. Leading the way in the semi-darkness, Jack turned a corner and went slap bang into a mountain goat. It was hard to tell who was the most surprised. Jack cursed and the goat let out a bleat. The goat was not alone, and soon the air was filled with a chorus of plaintive cries.

"Look at its ear!" exclaimed Bella excitedly. The others understood Bella's obsession with the eyelashes of the guanaco, but a goat's ear… could this be the first sign of madness?

"Look what is like stapled to its ear," repeated Bella. "Number 86."

"That's my number at school," said Ben.

"Where there's numbers, there are humans. Let's follow them."

Like the vicunas, the goats were quick and agile as they picked their way down the mountain, skipping from rock to rock. The leader of the herd, a black and white billy goat, had a bell around its neck. They followed the twinkling sound, and occasionally the dangling, silver bell glistened in the moonlight. They were blessed with a clear night and a full moon, and they were able to pick their way down in the silvery light. The lone, bright star had now been joined by a magnificent canopy of fellow stars. With the south cross at their back, they continued to clamber and stumble down, struggling to keep up with the pace of the goats.

"Look down in the bottom of the valley," pointed Jack excitedly. "Are those lights?"

They followed the direction of his finger, and there below was a cluster of lights nestling in the foothills of the valley.

"Those are no phantom lights," declared Bella, getting carried away in the excitement and starting to skip and sprint down the slope. Further down, the goats looked back at them, bemused by all the shouting and hollering.

After a two-hour descent, they finally arrived. The village, bathed in a silvery moonlight, was silent and appeared to be sleeping. The wooden houses, topped by glistening corrugated iron roofs, lined the single, dusty street. At intervals, in the windows, flickering fairy lights strung across fake plastic trees announced that it was Christmas. Flo was reminded of the poem, 'Silver', by Walter de la Mare;

'Slowly, silently, now the moon
Walks the night in her silver shoon;
This way, and that, she peers, and sees
Silver fruit upon silver trees;

One by one the casements catch
Her beams beneath the silvery thatch...'

At the far end of the high street, a light shone beckoning from the tower of a small, white-washed church. As they walked towards the church, silence continued to reign over the soulless houses and street. Suddenly, they heard the muffled rumble of chairs scraping on a hard stone floor, and then the singing 'Silent night' (in Spanish).

These were the first human voices they had heard for 14 days, and even though they were in a foreign language, the children had never heard words so beautiful.

Tentatively, they pushed open the arched oak doors. The creaking hinges announced their arrival to those sitting in the pews to the back of the packed church.

They turned, surprised, and immediately stopped singing, mouths hanging aghast at the sight of the four gringo children. They must have looked quite a sight. 14 days crossing Patagonia, surviving shipwreck, erupting volcanoes, living glaciers, storming grasshoppers and raging winds had taken their toll. Dishevelled, smelly and gaunt, the children stood silhouetted in the moonlight beyond the door. A Mexican wave of chatter and shoulder tapping spread down the wooden pews, and it was not long before the singing ground to a halt as the whole congregation turned their backs on the altar, and stared intently at their unexpected visitors. Last to turn was the cast of the nativity play surrounding the altar. There, centre stage, stood Joseph, in faded blue jeans, alongside a young Mary, dressed in a floral skirt and matching blouse. The three kings were distinguished by their brightly-coloured bobble hats, while the shepherds sported woollen hats without the bobbles.

With the singing stopped, silence reigned. Silence, as the congregation tried to make sense of the children's unexpected arrival. They were not used to visitors, situated as they were in the middle of nowhere, in Chile's far south. *Where had these children come from? Where were their parents?* The children in turn were asking very different questions. *Are these people friendly? Where are we? I wonder how we look?*

It was the teenage Joseph who broke the spell. He sauntered slowly down the aisle and gave Bella a big hug. Bella's blush and smile lit up the room. It was at this very moment, as the clock struck midnight, it dawned upon the children that they were safe and they had a Christmas to celebrate. Together, they had survived against all odds being Lost at the End of the World.

Epilogue – 10 years on...

All the children were now back from South America and all living in London. For the last three years, they had all been meeting up in a tapas bar, adorned with festive fairy lights, in Covent Garden on 23rd December, but today, at Jack's insistence, they were meeting for lunch at a Lebanese restaurant in South Kensington.

Jack, true to form, was the first to arrive. Now 26, he walked in with a calm self-assurance, gave his name to the waitress, and was ushered to a table for 4. He now had the job of his dreams as a wildlife cameraman for the BBC. He had just returned from filming gorillas in Rwanda for the latest David Attenborough documentary. He had loved the freedom and the solitary nature of the job – all alone with these fascinating creatures.

Next to arrive were Flo and Ben. Flo floated in serenely, while Ben walked in excitedly with that mischievous grin on his face. Flo was forging a career and reputation as a poet, and Ben was in his final year at school and planning to study Zoology at the University of York.

Needless to say, Bella was the last to arrive. She bustled and flustered in, apologising for being late but sporting a radiant smile. Her nose was no longer struck in air, and reassuringly her hair was messy and her complexion natural. Her clothes were casual and unfussy, and she was in her fourth year at Manchester studying to be a vet.

They all greeted each other like long-lost friends.

"Do you know," said Jack, "there is not a day that goes by that I do not think of our adventures in Patagonia?"

"Me too," agreed Bella. "Only today was I *not* thinking about waking up with a bunch of elephant seals."

"You're right!" said Ben excitedly. "Yesterday, I saw a tin of sardines and I thought of those grasshoppers." Bella winced.

"I wrote a poem the other day," said Flo, "about mystical rock formations in the desert."

"I'm not one for poetry, but I loved your poem about the ghost village. I wonder where you got your inspiration from?" teased Jack.

"Yes, that place was so spooky," confirmed Ben.

"That was my all-time low," said Bella. "Our hopes dashed, and it was then I thought there was no way out."

"Thank goodness for that. That is when you changed," said Flo. "Up until then you had been a complete pain in the backside." Bella nodded and laughed.

"Was I really that bad?" asked Bella.

"No, worse," ribbed Flo.

"That's harsh, sis," smiled Ben. "Bella did give me her sweater when I got really cold up that mountain."

"Patagonia did change me," said Bella. "I know I was a nightmare. Who files their nails in a storm and insists on taking their handbag on a life raft?"

"And says *'like'* every third word?" interrupted Flo, grinning. "Mercifully, you have stopped doing that."

"How are your parents?" asked Jack, changing the subject.

"We're on civil terms, but mainly they get on with their lives, and I get on with mine," replied Bella. "This does not upset me anymore. They don't approve of me becoming a vet, and I think this makes me the more determined."

"My father's the same," replied Jack. "He simply cannot understand why I would wish to spend hours on end in a jungle waiting to get just seconds of footage. Through my filming, I really feel that I have stepped out of his shadow. Where are your parents now?"

"Off skiing as usual," replied Bella. "It's Christmas in London for me."

"Alone?" asked Flo. Bella nodded.

"Come to ours," chorused Jack, Flo and Ben in unison.

"Fighting over me now," said Bella. They all laughed. "That is a turn up for the books. Do you know what, I might just do that."

"That's settled then. It is lunch at ours and dinner at Jack's," suggested Flo.

"We'll make sure all your favourite things are on the menu," teased Ben. "Penguin eggs and grasshoppers for starters and fairy armadillos with monkey puzzle pods as a main, and all finished off with tart, stringy, stewed rhubarb."

Bella made a face and then smiled. "Thanks for reminding me. I can hardly wait!"

"I often think about what would have happened if the *Maria Louise* had not sunk." mused Flo.

"Just have a look at us all. Here we all are pursuing and living our dreams," observed Jack.

He lifted his glass, "Here's to Patagonia, the land of dreams."

"And don't forget the extraordinary creatures and birds," interjected Flo.

"Now that reminds me," said Jack, with a mischievous grin. "I warned you that I had a surprise for you all."

"Go on," smiled Bella. "Gosh, how I used to hate surprises."

"Well, do you remember that claw, skin and dung we found in the Cave of Hands?" asked Jack.

"The monster cave more like," said Ben.

"Come on," said Flo, "stop keeping us all in suspense."

"I sent them to the Natural History Museum here in London," said Jack. "And today they have called us in to give us the results."

"So, 10 years on," said Ben, excitedly, "We finally get to find out whose home we shared in that cave!"

They filed into the Natural History Museum and they were ushered through a door that read 'No Public Access' to meet Professor Rawlings, a Palaeontologist.

"What's a Palaeontologist?" asked Ben.

"I think it's someone who specialises in dinosaurs," replied Jack.

A bearded Professor Rawlings rose to his feet to greet them.

"Please sit down," said the Professor. "Now I must say that these are the finest remains of a Mylodon I have ever seen." The children raised their eyebrows. "You may be more familiar with a Giant Sloth," he continued, helpfully.

"So we shared a cave with a Giant Sloth?" asked Ben, seeking clarification. "Are they dangerous?"

"Well, they might have been 12,000 years ago," replied the Professor.

"12,000 years ago?" exclaimed Jack, amazed. "The skin looked so fresh."

"Yes, that is why your find is so exciting," said the Professor. "The extreme cold and stable conditions in the cave must have kept them looking fresh."

"Well, that is Patagonia for you," said Ben.

"Yes… truly the most extraordinary place on earth," agreed the Professor.

Dear Reader, Next time you go to the Natural History Museum in London, look out for the claw the size of your hand, the skin with red fur and the spherical poo.

Afterword

I do hope that you have enjoyed following in the footsteps of Jack, Bella, Flo and Ben as they edged their way across the End of the World. I also hope that this book has sown the seed of adventure and left you dreaming about what a vast, amazing world we all live in. When your time is right, the possibilities to travel and explore are endless both close to home and further afield.

Some of you lucky ones might even find yourselves at the End of the World. It is truly a special place, which will inspire memories that will stay with you forever. Like Jack said in the final chapter, I also find that there is not a day that goes by without thinking about our adventures in Patagonia. Remember, it is not just about what you will see and experience, it is more about what you will learn about yourself...

List of Illustrators – 19 talented young artists

- Front cover – Virginia Manners
- Contents page – Ava Hitchins
- Cape Horn – Otto Gibbs
- Albatross – Virginia Manners
- Elephant Seal – Guy Palmer
- Group of Penguins – Molly Fletcher
- Single Penguin – Elsa Slettengren
- Cave of Hands – Grace Galvin
- Guanaco – Ollie Coombes
- Patagonian Mara – Aurea Urrutia
- Burrowing Owl – Florence Undery
- Condor – Will Fuller
- Rhubarb Forest – Evie Riley
- Alpacas – George Stanford
- Rheas – Antonio Perez-Maura Ruiz de Villa
- Abandoned Classroom – Florence Undery
- Rock Formations – Aurea Urrutia
- Armadillo – Freddie Smith
- Dinosaur Skeleton – Freddie Tregoning
- Grasshopper – Sam Shiel
- Horses – Amelia Blomfield
- Three Granite Towers – Olivia Cumming
- Vicuna – Evie Riley
- Lone Vicuna – Molly Fletcher
- Andean Church – Antonio Perez-Maura Ruiz de Villa

Acknowledgements

First of all, thank you to Patagonia for offering such a wonderful backdrop for a children's book. It is a truly unique, magical and beautiful place, and I feel immensely fortunate to have been there. I am not alone in loving this place, and I encourage all of you to visit one day – you will not regret it.

Thank you also to Michael Pask and David Nicholls, my cycling companions in Patagonia. Without them, I could not have endured the extreme elements and landscapes – the biting cold, the ferocious winds, the arid deserts, the desolate plains, the dizzy heights. Like the children, we learnt to relish these challenges and to become stronger for it. There is something of each of us in all four children, and their experiences mirror our own.

A huge thank you to all the pupils I have ever taught at Sandroyd School and Cothill House. They have been a constant encouragement and a sounding board when I have been struggling with the storyline. Sophie Welch and Natalie Galloway, in particular, helped me to find a way through the false dawn of the mining village. I also appreciated the infectious enthusiasm of Celine Cournil after reading the first draft.

Thank you also to Emmie Carson for taking the Year 7 budding artists under her wing and inspiring them to draw the wonderful illustrations for the book. The choice was truly overwhelming and thank you to all the pupils who took part. Virginia Manners designed the front cover, and a special mention goes to Florence Undery for her burrowing owl and abandoned classroom. The other 17 illustrators are listed overleaf and I am indebted to them all.

Being dyslexic, proofreading is often a challenge too far. I am thus very grateful to Helen Bussell, Simon Heazell and Olivia Cournil for patiently and diligently working their way through many inadvertent mistakes. Michael Mann was also a great help on advising the best route to publication.

As you can see, it was a real team effort and I am so thankful for everybody's support and encouragement.

Finally, a word of thanks to you, the reader, for picking up this book. I do hope you enjoyed the journey.

'Attlee can't just cycle, he can also write – this book is a rare treat'
THE MAIL ON SUNDAY
THE TRAIL TO TITICACA
A JOURNEY THROUGH SOUTH AMERICA
RUPERT ATTLEE

Also by the Author

It seemed like a mad enterprise: three inexperienced cyclists setting out to pedal 10,000 kms up the Andes, from Tierra del Fuego to Lake Titicaca. After nearly a year and against the odds – contending with grasshopper storms, deserts of volcanic ash and trigger-happy police – the trio succeeded in the objective, also raising tens of thousands of pounds for the Leukaemia Research Fund.

What started as an adventure of a lifetime evolved into a voyage of discovery, comradeship and humour.